BURNING DARKNESS

Jennifer Sights

ISBN: 978-0-9890838-6-7

This book is a work of fiction. Names, characters, places, and incidents either are products of the author's imagination or are used fictitiously. Any resemblance to actual persons, living or dead, events, or locales is entirely coincidental.

Author Info:
Website: http://www.JenniferSights.com
Facebook: http://www.facebook.com/JenniferSightsAuthor
Twitter: http://twitter.com/JenniferSights

ACKNOWLEDGEMENTS

I have to thank again, and always, my parents for all their support, and for working so hard to ensure I had the best life possible - a life the complete opposite of Basia's. Thanks to Chase Night for story consultation and Jason Whited for editing. Thanks to everyone who has bought my first two books and have told me how much they enjoy them. It means so much to hear that, and lets me know I'm doing something right. Thanks to everyone who has come to see me at conventions and talked to me about my books and writing in general.

Thanks to Michelle Benz for the amazing cover design. www. batspats.com

Thanks to Casey Carrington of Chalk & Soot for author photograph. www.chalkandsoot.com/index.html

CHAPTER 1

As Basia reached for consciousness, something in the back of her mind told her to stay in the blissful, peaceful darkness enveloping her. She sensed nothing good would come from being awake. She fought, trying to remain asleep, but the force working against her won.

She blinked a few times, then tried to rub her eyes, but she couldn't. Was she paralyzed? Anxiety began to seep in, so she forced herself to take slow, deep breaths. She wiggled her toes, then her fingers. No, not paralyzed. But why couldn't she move her arms and legs? Pressure on her wrists and ankles told her restraints held her down. If only it weren't so dark; if only she could see something, anything, maybe she'd be able to figure out where she was. She was trapped, in complete darkness, with no idea where she was or why. Panic took hold, and she screamed until her throat was raw, then continued screaming until she slipped back into unconsciousness.

When Basia woke, sun shone through the window. She looked around, taking stock of her surroundings. She was in some sort of hospital, though the other bed in her room was vacant. Silence permeated the building. Every time she'd been in a hospital to visit someone, the halls were filled with noises - doctors giving orders to the nurses, the beeping of various machines, the moaning of patients. Even in relatively quiet areas there was always noise. The hum of fluorescent lights, a TV with the nightly news, a daughter reading a book to her elderly father.

Sometimes, when Basia's head became too crowded, too much noise from the world scared her, inducing panic attacks. But now, the complete silence of this strange hospital was more terrifying than anything she had ever experienced.

Basia hoped she could remain calm enough to remember why she was here. She'd been doing so well; it had been weeks since her last attack. She'd worked too hard, for too long, to return to having multiple attacks in a day. If she was ever going to have a normal life, she had to be stronger than the anxiety.

But what was normal about waking up, strapped down to a bed in an abandoned hospital? She shouted for help, her throat still sore from screaming so much the night before, but she had to try to get someone's attention, had to find someone who would set her free. Why was she restrained? Weren't restraints for crazy people, people who were a danger to themselves or others? That wasn't her. Sure, sometimes the panic attacks made her feel like a danger to herself, but they were never anything that truly warranted restraints.

She realized there was a saline drip in her arm. The bag was nearly empty though, and how long would a saline drip really sustain her anyway if she didn't have real food and water? She had no idea. And couldn't the site of a needle puncture become infected if the needle was left in too long? It seemed as if that's something she'd overheard a nurse say when her mother was in the hospital all those years ago, but she couldn't be certain. That was an uncertain time, which had led to an even more uncertain life.

Basia tried to move her arms again but made no progress. Next, she wiggled her feet around, hoping for more leeway there. But there was no room to try to force her foot out. She was trapped.

A loud rumble from her stomach told her she needed to

eat. It hadn't even been a full day since she'd woken up in this place, but how long had she been there before that?

Are you sure you want to know the answer? a voice asked.

"Who's there?" Basia called out.

No one answered. Maybe she had imagined the voice.

Basia tried to think about the last thing she could recall, hoping to find an inkling of what had happened to her. She remembered working the closing shift at the restaurant, where a coworker had once again been taunting her about her panic attacks. She'd had another that night when a customer complained to her manager about her poor service. It hadn't been Basia's fault the cook screwed up the order, but the customer didn't care. He couldn't see the cook; Basia was an easier target. He was obviously the type of person who belittled other people as a method of making himself feel superior. That didn't ease Basia's mind though. She was only thankful she had made it to the break room before completely losing it.

But what had happened after that? She wracked her brain, trying desperately to remember. Sometimes, with a bad panic attack, she didn't remember what happened for a short while during and after. Had that been one of those nights? Surely, no one from the restaurant would have let her go home in that state.

Yes! Now she remembered. It had been a mild attack, and she had gone home as usual. But try as she might, she couldn't remember anything after that. When had that been? She had no way to find out.

CHAPTER 2

BASIA WIGGLED HER HANDS AND feet, hoping miraculously her bonds had somehow been loosened while she slept. She knew it was useless, but had to do something other than lie there, helpless.

To her surprise, she was able to work one hand free. The restraint had come loose from the bed itself. With a free hand it was easy to remove the other restraints. She pulled the needle out of her arm and held pressure on it until it stopped bleeding.

Panic crept in on her. Why should she panic now? She was free, she could go home now and get on with her life, and find out what had happened to her. She should have been more afraid when she was restrained and helpless, but something about the situation made freedom even more frightening, as if the stakes were raised. She had passed the first obstacle, but somehow knew the next would be even harder to overcome.

It will be harder than you can imagine.

Basia couldn't tell where the voice came from. It seemed to be all around her, yet inside her head at the same time. Even though she couldn't see anything, it was obvious there was no one else in the room. She would hear breathing, the small sounds people make just from being alive, clothing rustling with movement. When the voice was silent for several minutes, she decided to ignore it for the time being.

Clouds covering the moon denied her even a small bit of light in the dark building. She sat up and let her legs dangle over the bed, forcing herself to believe there was no monster waiting to grab her ankles and drag her into its lair. She forced herself to put her feet on the icy-cold tile floor and stand, then shuffled across the room in the direction she had seen the door in the daylight. She didn't pick her feet up for fear of stepping on or tripping over something.

When Basia finally reached the doorway, she realized she had no idea what was in either direction down the hall, or even what was in the hall. As much as she did not want to spend another night in the room, she realized it would be safer if she waited until she had some sunlight by which to explore. She shuffled back to the bed and tried to sleep. After minutes or hours, she finally did just that until the first rays of sun woke her and she could safely explore.

This time, she saw the hall was clear. Both directions looked the same, so she decided to go left, peeking into each doorway she passed. The hall was filled with rooms just like the one in which she had woken, each with two beds, each empty, clean and sterile. The place seemed to be abandoned, but it couldn't have been for long. It was far too clean. She couldn't even see any dust. To her horror, every single bed was equipped with restraints just like hers. Was it standard practice to strap the patients to their beds? She didn't know anything about insane asylums, but didn't think that was standard. Weren't patients only restrained if they were a danger to themselves or others? Surely, not that many dangerous people had been admitted here?

At the end of the hall she turned left, thinking it would be wise to make it easy to find her way back to her room. Basia shook her head at that thought. It wasn't her room, merely the room in which she had been imprisoned. She wasn't a patient; she was an inmate. Had the other people here been in the same situation as she? And where were they? Why was she the only one left behind?

Her grumbling stomach told her she needed to find the kitchen. Her mouth felt like cotton. So far, she hadn't come across any nurse's stations or sinks. That seemed odd. Weren't nurses and doctors always washing their hands? She didn't even see any of those little hand sanitizer dispensers. She hated that stuff. It smelled and made her hands dry. But she'd practically bathed in it every time she left her mother's hospital room, terrified of catching the disease that ate away at her mother.

Now she thought maybe it had been better if she had caught it and died too.

Two more turns brought her full circle back to her room. She could tell it was the room in which she'd woken because the sheets were mussed. All the other beds' sheets were neat and smooth, tucked in under the mattresses. She wished she could find a kitchen, and that there might be food in it.

Go downstairs, the voice said. Not having any better ideas, she searched for a stairwell and did just that. A keypad kept the door locked, but it had been disabled, allowing Basia easy access to the stairs. After searching a few hallways, she found the kitchen, and gulped water from the sink using her hands as a cup, her throat still sore from screaming.

No more screaming, she told herself. No more being a scared little child. It's time to grow up and take control of your life. Though she still wished her mother was there to hold her and tell her that the monsters weren't real. She knew they were real, though, and that it would never be okay again. And what made it even worse was the monsters looked just like her, and there was no way to tell them apart from the good guys.

A harsh lesson for a twelve-year-old to have had to learn.

After drinking her fill of water, Basia stood for a moment, wondering what was putting her ill at ease. Something was wrong. Something didn't fit.

She barked one harsh laugh at that thought. Nothing fit. But no, even in this strangeness, something else was wrong.

Humming. That's what it was. Electrical humming. She

walked slowly to the closest refrigerator, scared of the noise emanating from it. Why was there electricity in the kitchen but nowhere else she'd been so far? She put the palm of her hand flat against the side of the refrigerator, feeling its coolness and the slight vibration from the electricity running through it. Looking behind the machine, she saw a power cord plugged into the wall, but there was a box fashioned around it so it could not be unplugged. Strange.

Yet again her stomach grumbled, so she tossed aside her apprehension and opened the refrigerator doors, hoping there was something inside she could eat. What she saw was heaven. Fruit, vegetables, salad dressing, pasta sauce, hamburger, sandwich meat...she may as well have been in a miniature supermarket. There was more food than she'd be able to eat in a month, providing it didn't spoil before she got to it.

Of course it would spoil before she ate it. She was going to get out of here, she reminded herself.

But what if you don't?

Again Basia couldn't tell if the voice was her own thoughts, or something external to her. She shook her head and tried to forget it.

And why is there such good food here?

Basia thought about that. Hospital food was awful. She'd never seen anything as wonderful as what was in that fridge on a hospital tray. It made no sense.

She made herself a sandwich and devoured it, then half of another. When her hunger was satisfied, she looked around, hoping to find something she could use as a weapon. She didn't know why she needed a weapon. It was obvious no one else was there with her. Well, aside from the mysterious voice. But a weapon likely wouldn't help against that.

After searching every cabinet and drawer in the kitchen, she didn't find a single knife. They must have been locked up somewhere in case a patient got loose.

No matter. It was time to find the door and get the hell out of there. Every time she saw a window, it was barred, which made sense. The patients were there for a reason, and shouldn't be able to get out to further harm themselves.

But she wasn't crazy. There was no reason for her to be there. It was okay for her to leave.

Finally she found the entrance to the building. Two heavy steel doors in a large atrium. There was no handle on the doors, so they must open toward the outside of the building. When she pushed against them, they didn't even budge. No rattle, nothing. It was as if the doors were sealed shut. She saw no way to open them. Why would someone do that? Hadn't they known she was in there? There had to be another way out.

Forcing herself to remain calm, she tried to think. Running around like a madwoman was no way to find an escape. She had to be methodical about this. She had to find a map of the building, a floor layout, so she could find her way around and systematically check every floor and room so she didn't waste time retracing her steps in this maze of an asylum.

CHAPTER 3

CALM DOWN AND THINK LOGICALLY, Basia told herself. You're at the main entrance of this hell hole. Surely there's an admin office nearby. She looked to either side of the atrium - what kind of insane asylum had an atrium anyway? Wasn't that reserved for fancy hotels? A door that looked promising stood to the right. Of course, it was locked. Luckily though, it had a glass window at the top of it, like in school rooms. She went to the nearest patient room she could find, yanked the sheets off the bed, and wadded them up to protect her elbow when she smashed out the window. She was just barely able to reach her arm down to unlock the door and let herself in. Not as smart as they think they are, she thought at how easily she had gotten past the lock.

It was darker in the office as there were no windows to the outside. She searched through the drawers by feel, hoping to find a flashlight. She didn't find one, so she took a stack of papers from one of the drawers out into the atrium where she could see better. There was nothing helpful there, so she returned them to their original place and grabbed a few more.

After an hour of searching through papers from the office in this manner, she finally found a layout of the building.

When she made her way across the building to the utility closet, she was thankful to find a large flashlight along with spare batteries. Things were looking up. She was also grateful it was a Maglite, which could double as a weapon should she need to protect herself from something, though she was thinking that was less and less likely.

The monsters will come for you whether or not you have light, the voice reminded her, echoing off the walls of the hallway and the inside of her head.

After surveying the room for anything else that might be useful and finding nothing - though she noted a large tool box - she grabbed as many batteries as she could carry and went back to the kitchen to formulate a plan.

Even though she now had a flashlight, she still didn't like the idea of exploring the building in the dark. It scared her. She'd always been afraid of the dark, ever since... And this silent dark was worse than most darks. She decided to wait out the night and start searching the building first thing the next morning.

When the sun rose, she started back at the atrium, this time going to the opposite side from the office she'd explored the day before. Again she had to break a window to get into the room. Not very secure, she thought. This time she wondered if it wasn't meant to be. This room had a barred window to the outside so it was easier to search. Still, it yielded nothing useful except for a binder that had the name of the place on the front; *Stockhill Asylum.*

As much as she wanted to sprint ahead to what looked to be a storage area according to the map, she forced herself to search each room in order that she didn't lose track of her progress. More administrative offices with no useful papers, a common room at either end of the building, and lots of patient rooms in between were all she found. The only thing useful in all the upper floors was the storage room, where she was ecstatic to find scrubs stacked on shelves. She also found a robe to help keep her warm, though it had no sash with which to tie it. She supposed that was so the patients couldn't try to hang themselves.

She also had failed to find any unbarred windows to the outside or doors that would lend an escape.

On the third day after waking up, Basia knew she'd have to search the basement. She didn't want to go down there. And when she tried, the door was locked. This was a very solid steel door without a window. Still, it had hinges just like all doors. She went back to the utility closet and grabbed some screw drivers and a hammer, and set to work at getting the heavy door off its hinges. She almost dropped it on herself when it finally came free, but she managed to jump to the side just in time to let it crash safely, but loudly, to the floor.

Good thing you didn't crush yourself. Would have been such a waste.

Basia was no closer to figuring out where the voice was coming from, but had grown better at ignoring it. She refused to answer anything it said, fearing that would mean she really was crazy.

Making sure she had spare batteries, she crept down the stairs, having no idea what to expect at the bottom, but half expecting some kind of vicious monster.

Habit made her flip the light switch at the bottom of the stairs a couple of times, to no avail. She shone the light around and saw that the basement was empty. But far off to the back she saw a door with a heavy padlock on it. She laughed in defiance. What good would a padlock do against her growing breaking-and-entering skills? Prepared to take another door off its hinges, she walked across the long length of the open basement. When she got to the door, though, she realized it would prove more difficult, for it had no hinges. It appeared to be a sliding door, set an inch back in the wall. She would have to figure out how to get the padlock off.

She tried breaking it with the hammer, but it was too thick. Basia knew this room had something that would help her. If not an escape route, information to help her understand what was going on. Perhaps this was the room to which all the files had been moved. She hoped she'd find something in the utility closet to help her get through the padlock.

You shouldn't be here. The voice was louder and more adamant than previously.

"Who are you?"

You shouldn't be here, the voice repeated.

"No kidding. That's why I'm trying to find a way out."

You shouldn't be here.

"If you're so adamant about that, why don't you help me get out of here?"

There is only one way out.

"So where is it?"

All you have to do is look.

"I have been looking, and I haven't found anything yet. I need to get through this locked door."

After waiting a few minutes for an answer, Basia made her way back to the stairs to search the utility closet for something useful. She found a pair of bolt cutters that looked substantial, and she hoped it would be enough to get through the padlock. She had no idea how to pick a lock, so if these didn't work, she didn't know what else to do.

She hurried back to the basement. The bolt cutters just fit around the padlock, but she wasn't quite strong enough to cut through. She needed better leverage somehow. She tried holding one handle against the door with her hand and tried to get the right angle to kick the other handle. After many tries, she finally got it right and broke through.

You shouldn't be here.

"If that's all you're going to say, you can just shut up," Basia said, annoyed at not knowing where the voice was coming from.

The door slid easily into the wall, almost silently, except for the soft bang it made when it reached the end of the track. The room behind the door was smaller than the rest of the basement, and the walls were lined with boxes of files stacked four high. Jackpot! Basia looked around some more, and was ecstatic to see a manhole cover right in the middle of the floor. Finally, a way out. She was torn though - did she want to get the hell out of there, or did she want to search through the files in hopes of finding some clue as to what had happened to her and why she was there?

She decided on at least exploring the escape route first. She could always come back for the files. After shining the flashlight down the hole and confirming that there was, in fact, a ladder, Basia lowered herself down. It was tricky with the flashlight in her hand. She had to hook her elbow over the rungs so as not to drop it. Every few rungs she shone the flashlight down, and finally was able to see the bottom. She stepped into water about two inches deep and groaned. "Gross." Well, no use giving up now, her feet were already soaked in whatever filth the water contained.

She walked for about fifteen minutes and found no sign of any exits. That's when she heard a dull roar from the direction of the ladder. She didn't know what it was, but something told her to go back the way she came. She ran back to the ladder and made it in almost half the time. Just as she started climbing, a wall of water hit her. The sewer was being flooded. Thank goodness she'd made it to the ladder and was able to hang on, and climb back up. She didn't want to think what might have happened to her otherwise.

Well, there was more waiting she'd have to do. To be safe, she knew it was best if she watched for when the water went down, and waited to see when it filled back up again, so that she'd know how long she had the next time she ventured down. At least she knew what she was up against now.

CHAPTER 4

AFTER A TEDIOUS TWENTY-FOUR hours of watching the sewer, Basia was disheartened by what she'd discovered. There was only a single one hour period each day during which the tunnel was not flooded. That meant she only had thirty minutes to go in either direction before having to turn back for safety. Thankfully, running was one of her hobbies. A necessity, really. She hadn't been able to get away from him as a child, and as soon as she was physically able, had promised herself she'd never be vulnerable like that again.

A day later, after ensuring she was fully rested, Basia ventured down into the sewer. She started when the water was still over her ankles, buying a few extra minutes of exploration time. She'd taken a small, battery powered clock from one of the office desks and periodically shone the flashlight on it to check how much longer she had.

She walked a quick pace for forty minutes and didn't find a single exit. She knew she had to turn around and jog back. She was almost to the ladder when she heard the roaring, and again was soaked as she started to climb back up.

Basia went to change into dry clothes and take a nap. It had obviously been a while since she'd jogged, and the twenty-minute run had worn her out. After having a sandwich for dinner, she went back to the basement to search through the boxes of files.

The boxes were labeled in the way she'd seen patient files labeled in doctor offices - with the first two letters of the last name. Unfortunately, the boxes weren't in order, so it took her a while to find the box where her file should be. She thumbed through it, and of course there wasn't one for her in the box.

"A little help right now would be nice," she said aloud in case the mysterious voice was listening. But nothing happened, so she started at one end of the stacks of boxes and started looking through each and every one, hoping to find a file on herself in there. She was thumbing through the first box in the fifth stack when her eyes started to droop. She didn't want to stop, but knew if she didn't there was a good chance she'd miss what she was looking for. She sighed, and headed upstairs to sleep.

Don't stop now, you're closer than you think, the voice finally said.

"You couldn't have done this hours ago before I was damn near falling asleep on my feet?" She tried to ignore the voice and kept walking.

You're making a mistake. Don't stop now, the voice shouted loud enough to hurt her ears.

"All right, stop it! I'm going back. Just stop already," she said.

The air pushed her to a box in the opposite corner from where she'd started. "How did I miss that?" she wondered aloud. She opened the box, and there was only one file in it. That file had her name on the tab and was about an inch thick. She wondered why her file was so much thicker than the others she'd gone though, but was thankful she wouldn't have to spend any more time in the cold basement.

Suddenly wide awake again and eager to start reading, Basia dragged a bed so it was in a ray of sunshine coming through the window. She'd already gone through one set of batteries for the flashlight and didn't want to waste any more. She flipped open the cover and the first page had a picture of her paper clipped to it. It was her high school graduation picture. She hadn't had any others taken since then. Taking pictures was something friends and family did. She no longer had either.

Basic stats filled the page - age, height, hair and eye color, weight, address, place of employment. She flipped to the next page which followed her life history from where she was born, to her father's death, then her mother's. She read the first half of the file, crying at the memories it brought up that she'd tried so hard to bury.

July 17, 2002

Basia shows signs of depression and delusion. She still speaks to her father as if he is there. It is similar to young children speaking to imaginary friends, but she should have outgrown that phase. When asked who she is talking to, she says "Daddy" in a tone that indicates she thinks I am stupid for asking, as if I should see him as well. I asked if she is pretending to talk to him, and she said no, that he was right there. This led me to ask if she was talking to his ghost, and she shook her head without even looking at me, clearly done with the conversation.

Basia was ten years old in 2002, and July was only two months after her mother had married Dr. James Godfrey. He had seemed nice enough, but Basia didn't want a new daddy. She didn't recall the event chronicled in her file, didn't recall ever talking to her father after his death. Sure, she'd been depressed for quite a while, but what little girl wouldn't be when her father was stolen from her at such a young age?

Reading further she discovered more events similar to the first one. She assumed they had been written by Dr. Godfrey - she had called him James when she lived with him, but refused to use anything so cordial in reference to him now. He was a psychiatrist, so perhaps it made sense that he had kept notes on her, maybe to assist with the grieving process, but why would they be here? He'd moved halfway across the country last she checked.

She flipped ahead, and saw pages and pages more of notes in the same handwriting. The date on the last handwritten one was from 2008.

April 28, 2008
Basia still hasn't been found after running away from Susan and Gary last week. She doesn't have many friends, and the ones we know of haven't seen her. The police are looking, and she's been added to the missing children registry. We are worried about her.

That much was true. Basia had run away from her aunt and uncle's house the day she turned sixteen. She knew she could petition for emancipation, but also knew her chances of success were slim. Dr. Godfrey had legally adopted her two years after he married her mother, and very reluctantly agreed to let her live with her aunt and uncle after her mother died. She knew he was very influential, and that he'd convince the authorities not to give her what she wanted. So she spent two years living on the streets, in homeless shelters when she could, and only when she turned eighteen was she able to start working a legitimate job, without fear of Dr. Godfrey finding her and forcing her back into his household.

It hadn't been easy, and Basia had done plenty of things she was ashamed of in those two years. But it was easier than what Dr. Godfrey subjected her to, even after she'd moved out of his house.

When his notes ended, typed notes began. They followed Basia's life from age eighteen to now, four years later. They were less detailed than the handwritten notes, probably because Dr. Godfrey had moved away and wasn't able to easily spy on Basia anymore. But if he had moved to California as she thought he had, how had he known anything about her? Had he asked someone else to do his dirty work? That was entirely possible. He had been very well connected in the medical community, even in a city as small as Columbia, Missouri.

That thought chilled Basia more than whatever it was that might be in the asylum with her. How had she been spied on for four years and not had any idea? Then again, she hadn't been looking for it. She thought once she'd turned eighteen and Dr. Godfrey had moved two thousand miles away she would be safe from him. Boy, had she been wrong.

The typed notes contained details about her job and where she lived, and even notes about the few coworkers she managed to have real conversations with. That meant the person had been in the restaurant, on a regular basis. How else would the person know who she talked to at work?

November 14, 2012
Observed Basia at La Terraza Grill today. She was more withdrawn than usual, giving the customers the minimum required attention. I arrived halfway through her shift, ensuring I was seated in a different section than the one she was working to avoid detection, though I think she was too much in her own head to have noticed me anyway. I'm not sure she truly saw any of her customers. Shortly after I arrived, she asked the manager for a ten-minute break, during which she retreated into the bathroom and did not emerge until the end of the break. I wonder what happened to make her so much more withdrawn than usual. It would be ideal if we had more complete access to her life.

Basia flipped through the rest of the file and saw it contained similar entries, with enough detail on her life to give her chills. When she finished, there were still a few hours before the tunnel would be clear again. She was afraid if she slept she wouldn't wake up in time, so decided to have something to eat while she waited. When the water finally receded enough for her to climb down, she walked in the opposite direction as she had the last time. She didn't jog to begin with so she wouldn't have to worry about missing a potential exit, and wanted to conserve her energy for the return run back to the ladder should she fail to find a way out.

As had happened last time, she found nothing even remotely resembling an exit in her forty minutes of walking. Just as she was about to turn around and start the run back, she thought she saw a glimmer of light. Basia turned off the flashlight and stood with her eyes closed for a few seconds, willing them to adjust to the darkness. When she opened them again, she at first saw nothing but black. But then she saw just a glimmer of light, far off in the distance. It might have just been her imagination, and she didn't have time to investigate. As it was, she had already wasted too much time. She'd have to run faster than ever to make it back to the ladder before the wall of water swept her away.

Basia's lungs burned when she heard the roaring ahead her. She pushed herself faster, her legs feeling like rubber that would give out at any moment. The first rush of water gathered around her ankles, making every step precarious as the rushing water threatened to sweep her off her feet. The beam from the flashlight bounced up and down, but she saw the ladder in the distance.

The water rose higher and was around her knees by now. Basia could no longer run, only wade as quickly as possible. The ladder was mere feet away now, but may as well have been miles. Four feet. Three feet. Two feet. She reached out and grabbed the ladder, knowing it was all over.

Somehow, she managed to hold on in the blackness of rushing water, which now covered her head. Her lungs screamed for oxygen. With all her might, she held on with both hands, slowly working her way up the ladder, terrified each time she had to let go with one hand to reach for the next rung. Lights flashed behind her eyelids, and she knew she was close to losing consciousness from lack of oxygen, or even worse, close to gasping in a giant lungful of water.

She was so tired, so weak. She wanted to just give up. What did she have to live for anyway? A meaningless job as a waitress, no friends, no direction in life, nothing but more panic attacks. Yes, it would be easier to just let go.

The moment before Basia did just that, she felt air on her face. The darkness was still complete, but she knew she'd made it into the small space between the tunnel proper and the exit to the asylum basement. With one last renewed rush of energy, she pulled herself up out of the hole and onto the cold concrete floor. She knew she risked hypothermia lying there in nothing but wet scrubs, but she had no energy to move another millimeter. She let herself slip into unconsciousness on the cold, hard floor at the edge of the hole to the sewer.

CHAPTER 5

BASIA WOKE UP, WARM. HER body ached from the hard concrete floor of the basement, and she had no idea what time of day or night it was. What had happened? She lay still for a few moments gathering her memories. Oh yes, the rushing water that had almost drowned her. She'd lost her precious flashlight. She'd almost died. But here she was, alive and somehow warm. Why was she so warm? She should have been freezing. When the water hadn't killed her, the cold of the basement should have. But here she was.

She wiggled her toes, happy they were still there and mobile. As she worked her way up her body, flexing muscles, the warmth receded. It was as if an invisible blanket had been covering her, and disappeared now that she no longer needed it. This was too weird. She didn't even bother to try to figure that one out. She had to find her way out of the basement and to warmth. She stood and stretched, happy to discover her body didn't seem to be too much worse for the wear. She had no idea which way the door was, so she walked straight with her hands out in front of her until she found a wall. She made her way around the room until she found the door, then tried to walk in as straight a line as possible.

After what seemed like ages, she finally found the stairs to the upper floors of the asylum. Tired of being in the dark, she prayed for daylight.

The last rays of the sun were sinking below the windows as Basia made it to the top of the stairs. She rushed to the nearest patient room and burrowed under the blankets, suddenly more afraid than she had been since she'd woken in that terrible place, reverting to the childhood misbelief that if she hid under the covers the monsters wouldn't find her.

You know better than most that hiding under the blankets won't save you from the monsters. You know that's where they like you best, Basia heard as she drifted to sleep.

In her dream, Basia thought she saw the outline of a person, a girl perhaps, though it was hard to tell in the dark. The figure seemed to be illuminated from within, but just enough to make her question whether she really saw anything or if it was just her mind playing tricks on her.

Reaching out for the girl, trying to walk closer to her, Basia felt as if she was walking on a conveyer belt, getting nowhere. She called out to the misty girl, but got no reply. Suddenly, the girl glowed brighter and brighter until Basia had to close her eyes against the brilliance.

She woke up to the sun shining on her face, relieved to finally be able to see something again. Throwing the covers off, she went to find some clean clothes in the storage closet. She should just stack them all up in the room she had claimed as her own until she was able to escape. But the extra exercise was good for her, so she didn't.

Once she was in clean clothes, she went to make some breakfast, then hunted for another flashlight and more batteries. She found plenty more batteries, but no sign of another flashlight. Scouring the kitchen, however, yielded a few candles. Why on Earth would there be candles in a place like this? Surely they didn't have candlelit dinners for the patients? She let the question go, grateful for any sort of light.

Before going for what she hoped would be her last trip into the sewer tunnel, Basia wrapped her file in cling wrap from the kitchen many times. She sealed it in a Ziploc bag, wrapped that in cling wrap, and sealed it in a second Ziploc bag. She wanted to be sure the file would survive if she met another tidal wall of water before she safely made her escape. She knew if she left the file behind her chances of ever retrieving it were slim.

She was as ready as she was going to get. She thought about going down when the water was still at waist depth, but decided against using her energy to wade through the water. She would need all the strength she could muster to make it to the source of the light in the short time she had. She also found some tape to secure the bundle to her body, underneath her shirt, so she wouldn't have to worry about carrying it.

She walked down to the basement and waited at the edge of the entrance to the sewer tunnels by the light of a candle. She quickly realized a candle wasn't a realistic lighting option to carry while she was running through the tunnel. Well, there was only one choice. She would have to explore the sewer tunnel in the dark, running toward the light she thought she'd seen as fast as she could and hope that it was an exit. There was nothing else to do besides sit and rot in this awful place.

When the water started receding she climbed partway down the ladder, candle in hand. She wanted to be able to see exactly when it was safe to take the final steps down. As soon as it was, she dropped the candle into the inch-deep water and took off running as fast as she could in the direction she'd seen the glimmer of light.

She ran and ran, gasping for breath, wishing it hadn't been so long - how long had it been? - since she'd trained. She'd always wanted to run a marathon, but social anxiety prevented her from doing it every time she decided to try. She forced herself to keep running, knowing it was her only chance. If she didn't find an exit before the tunnel filled again, it was all over for her.

Finally, she saw the light in the distance and let out a whoop of elation. It hadn't just been her imagination! She pushed herself to keep going and the light grew larger and brighter. She squinted as her eyes adjusted to the new blessing of something other than blackness and kept going. As she grew even closer, she saw it was indeed an opening at the end of the tunnel, but that the opening was covered by three-inch-thick bars spaced just close enough that she couldn't squeeze through.

Basia looked around the area she could see from the illumination. There was a ladder going up. Escape! She scrambled up the ladder and tried to push the manhole cover aside, but it was stuck. No matter how hard she tried, she couldn't get it to budge.

You thought you were going to escape. That's funny. I think you're just going to die here.

"Shut up!"

Laughter filled Basia's head.

Climbing back down, she looked out the tunnel exit. It looked as if it led to some sort of water plant. She didn't know why the tunnel would be empty for an hour each day. Maybe some sort of maintenance window? It didn't matter, she only had a few minutes left before it filled again, and no way to escape. She'd have to figure out how to weather the next twenty-three hours.

There wasn't time to run back to the asylum, not without risking being swept off her feet. She knew the water flowed much faster than she could run, and she was already tired from the sprint here. She climbed back up the ladder, and hunched while the tunnel filled. The power of the water terrified her. She hadn't had time to really think about it the last time she'd been caught up in it, but now, having nothing to do other than wait, she realized how powerful it was.

She had to get the manhole cover open. She braced her feet against the ladder as well as possible and pushed. It didn't even budge. She kept trying though, and when she thought she had no more strength left, gave one last push with a scream of frustration, and finally managed to get it free, allowing her to climb out to freedom.

Basia looked around her and realized she was, in fact, near

a water treatment plant. A fence topped with barbed wire was just ten feet away. She hoped no one had seen her climb out of the sewer. Looking in every direction, she was thankful not to see anyone. That didn't mean there weren't security cameras monitoring the perimeter though, so she decided she'd better get as far away as fast as possible.

So you didn't die in there after all. I'm surprised.

It sounded like something Basia might say to herself, making her further doubt whether it was a voice in her own head, or something external. She wished it would stop, but didn't know what do to about it.

She walked for miles, not knowing which direction she should go. She didn't know where she was, or if she was even still in Columbia. She had started walking around the perimeter of the water treatment plant, hoping to see a sign, but before she could make it all the way around, she heard voices. She knew it was too dangerous to have an encounter with anyone in her current state, so she ran off into the surrounding woods and didn't turn back. Going on the assumption she was still in Columbia - for what else could she do? She had to start somewhere - she headed east toward town. It was chilly outside and Basia was weary of being cold all the time. If she hadn't lost too much time it would be mid-April.

After miles and miles, Basia finally saw that she was indeed still in Columbia. She oriented herself, and waited until dark to walk the rest of the way to her apartment. She thought about going to the police, but if Dr. Godfrey was involved with this crazy situation, the police might bring her straight to him instead of helping her.

When she got to her block, she saw that going into her apartment wasn't an option. Someone was in there, someone she didn't recognize. Was it a burglar? She watched a few minutes, and saw that the person looked very at home. Had her apartment been rented out to someone else?

How long had she been gone?

Basia resigned herself to the fact that she had no other option than to go to the police. The front desk clerk stared when she walked through the door. "Can I get your name?" she asked, voice shaking, as the color drained from her face.

"Basia Reed," she said, chest tightening because of the way the clerk behaved.

"Please, come with me." The clerk led Basia to a small room that might have been an office, but held no personal items to show whom the office might belong to. "Someone will be right with you," she said, then closed the door behind her as she left.

Slow, deep breaths helped stave off a panic attack, but just barely. A few more minutes alone and she wouldn't have been able to fight it any longer, but a police officer came in before panic took hold.

"Hello Basia, I'm Officer Eric Smith. Can I get you anything to drink?"

"Just water, I guess."

Officer Smith returned a few minutes later with a bottle of water for Basia and Styrofoam cup of cup of coffee for himself, then sat across the table from her. "Now, Basia, can you tell me what happened to you?"

"I don't understand what's going on. What day is it?"

"April 19."

Basia thought back. "Wait...the last day I remember working was April 27. How can it possibly be the nineteenth?"

Officer Smith paused and took a sip of coffee. "There's no good way to say this, so I'll just say it. You were reported missing almost a full year ago, Basia."

Chest tightening, panic finally took hold, and Basia couldn't breathe. She tried to control her breath, but the battle was already lost. Her vision blurred, and she slipped into unconsciousness.

Opening her eyes, Basia found herself lying on a cold tile floor. Paramedics hovered over her and took her vitals once she was awake. They left when they were confident everything was back to normal.

"Would you like to take a shower in the locker room, Basia?" Officer Smith asked. "I can find some spare sweatpants and a T-shirt for you."

"That would be wonderful, thanks," she said, wanting nothing more than to get out of the filthy scrubs and into clean, warm clothes. She felt better, stronger, after the shower, and more ready to tell Officer Smith what had happened to her.

"Before we start, I want to let you know your stepfather is on his way here."

"What?" Basia's eyes widened.

"Dr. Godfrey. He's been very worried about you since you went missing. When I called to tell him you were here he said he'd be on the first flight possible so he could take care of you."

"No, that can't be." Basia shook her head.

"What's wrong, Basia?" Officer Smith asked.

"He can't come here. He - I don't want to see him."

"Well he's on his way. It will probably be early tomorrow before he makes it to town."

"No, he's done horrible things to me. I ran away from home for a reason when I was a kid."

"I'm sorry, Basia, but he said you have no friends, and you'll need someone to help you recover from whatever you experienced. Can you tell me about that?"

Basia stood. "No, I can't stay here, he can't find me."

"Please, sit down. We need to know what happened to you so we can help you."

"If I tell you, will you let me leave before he gets here?"

"We can't make you stay. You aren't under arrest for anything."

Basia sat back down. "Fine. I'll tell you, but then I'm leaving." She told Officer Smith what little she remembered as quickly as possible. When she finished, she stood and walked out of the room before he could ask any questions. Once out of the building, she ran as fast as she could, thankful it was still dark so she wouldn't be easy to follow.

CHAPTER "6"

BASIA WORRIED THE POLICE WOULD chase her, so she didn't stop to think where she should go. She didn't know where to go anyway, so she just ran.

Relief flooded her when she realized she had subconsciously been running in the direction of the university. It would be easy to hide there on campus. She could blend in with the college students, maybe even duck into the library.

When she was confident she wasn't being followed, that's exactly what she did. She weaved in and out of shelves of books, walked up to the second floor and wandered some more, just to be absolutely certain she was alone. Finally, she found a chair in a dim corner and sat.

She didn't know how long she had until the library closed. What the hell had happened to her in the past year? Why couldn't she remember anything? Had she been kidnapped? Or had she simply disappeared? Well, that would explain why her apartment had been rented out to someone else.

No one gave her a second glance, so she decided to make use of what time she had at the library. She searched for the library's hours and was happy to see it was open until 2:00 a.m. She had no idea it would be open that late, but it certainly made things easier for her. Already, the wheels were turning on how she could get herself out of this mess. And how to find out exactly what this mess was.

If she could continue to blend in as a student, she'd be able to spend much of her time in the library tracking down Dr. Godfrey and who might be working for him. She had to figure out where she'd been. She pulled up an aerial map of Columbia and started at the water treatment plant. From there, she scanned the surrounding area for large buildings until she found something that looked like it might be a hospital. It didn't take her long to find what she thought must be Stockhill Asylum, though it wasn't labeled on the map.

Next, Basia ran a search on Stockhill Asylum. Hundreds of pages of results came back. She knew she was going to need a way to take notes, and she didn't trust any sort of online document storage, even if she did sign up under a fake name. Something told her she was part of something bad and that she shouldn't trust anyone or anything.

Too bad you didn't realize that before you so stupidly went running to the police.

She deleted her search history and closed the browser window, knowing she couldn't be too careful. After grabbing several sheets of used pieces of paper from a recycling bin and a stray pen, she went back to the computer and ran her search again. She took pages of notes on the sinister history of Stockhill Asylum.

The place had been an insane asylum for ages. Built in the late 1800s, it had been a place of horror, where cruel experiments had been run on the inmates. Inmates, not patients, for once one was admitted to Stockhill Asylum, they were never released. Back then, people still believed mental illness was the work of the devil and that even if one did appear to be cured, they were never believed to be completely well, and were thought to be an eternal threat to the safety and sanity of those around them.

Perfectly sane people were sent to the asylum as well, mostly women, simply because they didn't stand up to societal expectations. Women who were a little too interested in their sensual side, women who thought, women who didn't want to marry, women who spoke out against men...the list went on.

The asylum was closed in 1940 and remained vacant for over forty years. In the mid-1980s it was completely renovated and reopened under the name Stockhill Institute for Mental Health.

That made Basia stop. Why did the binder she had found read Stockhill Asylum then? Why would they put the old name on the newly opened hospital? Was it some sick joke one of the staff had thought funny? Or was it some sort of a message to her?

"Yessssss," a voice whispered behind her.

She whipped around in her chair, but no one was there. She stood and peeked around the nearest bookshelves but was alone. Basia rubbed her eyes. She'd have to figure out a place to sleep soon. There was a small homeless shelter on the outskirts of the city that she had volunteered at a few times when her social anxiety wasn't getting the best of her. She dismissed that thought. The police might have put out a notice about her and would surely have included the shelter since she had no home anymore. She'd have to tough it out on the streets somewhere.

After folding up her notes, she stuck them in the bag with the papers from her file from the asylum. She refused to call it a mental hospital. From the moment she'd woken up, she knew there was something wrong with the place. She had to learn more about it, but the library was going to close soon, and she didn't want to arouse suspicion by being the last person to leave. She slipped out the front door and headed across campus, not sure where she was going to spend the rest of the night.

Basia woke stiff the next morning. She'd slept leaning against a tree deep within Capen Park, which butted up to the University of Missouri campus. It had been cold, uncomfortable, and downright frightening, but was the best she could come up with.

She was starving, and knew she was going to have to rely on her old skills of thievery to survive for a while. She hated that, but didn't know what else to do. When she'd first run away at sixteen, she learned the tricks of blending in at hotel lobbies to snag something from the continental breakfast spread and how to snatch fruit from farmer's markets without being noticed. She hoped her skills weren't too rusty. Given the option, she'd rather starve than be caught stealing and have the police pick her up, at least until she knew what was going on.

After cleaning up as much as possible in a gas station bathroom and finding a somewhat busy hotel lobby from which to snag some food - two bagels and a couple pieces of fruit would do nicely to last the day - she went back to the library on campus to continue her research.

She searched recent articles for Stockhill Institute for Mental Health and saw that the place had shut down just last year after some sort of scandal. Details were sketchy, but she gathered it had something to do with a misdiagnosed patient who died after being given too much of the wrong drugs. Once that patient's family sued, several other families followed, and the institute was forced to close. While two of the doctors were put on trial, they were acquitted, thanks to the sorry state of mental health and the grossly misunderstood symptoms. It was so hard to properly diagnose anyone that sometimes these things just happened, according to the lawyers.

The asylum had closed approximately one month prior to the last day Basia remembered anything.

Next, she searched for what she could find on doctors associated with the hospital, and whom those doctors associated with. It was a long, twisted line that one had to be looking closely for, otherwise it would be easily missed, but after hours of searching she finally managed to tie Dr. Godfrey to a man named Dr. Leon Schultz, one of the doctors who had worked at the institute.

That gave her all the proof she needed that he was involved. But of course she'd need something more concrete than a gut feeling and a convoluted list of doctors to convince anyone else. Dr. Godfrey had won awards for his work in the mental health field and had been on a congressional committee about the state of mental health in the United States, invited by the president himself. It would take perfect, airtight evidence to bring him down.

She gathered her notes and left the library. She wanted to spread out her time there so she wouldn't be too conspicuous. She'd have to check out the public libraries as well and see how their Internet access was set up so she wouldn't spend too much time in any one place. Before leaving, she made sure to clear the browser history again. She figured it was probably stored somewhere else she couldn't access, but she did what she could to cover her tracks.

She walked around campus, thankful it was spring and not too terribly cold, stopping at the student union where she sat down to read a magazine someone had left behind.

That's when she felt someone watching her. She looked around but didn't see anyone who appeared to be taking any extra interest in her. Even so, she decided she should get out of there and head somewhere else.

Trying to appear casual, she walked back outside. Only then did she notice the tall, gangly boy with shaggy hair and baggy skater clothes watching her. Had he been leaning against that wall the entire time? If so, why hadn't she noticed him earlier? She tried to ignore him and act like she wasn't in high-alert paranoid mode. She walked out the door and down the steps of the castle-like building and then turned right at the bottom. As she did, she tried to casually glance to see if the boy was following her, and heaved a sigh of relief to see he was not. Just to be safe, she took a few random turns before leaving campus.

CHAPTER 7

As Basia left the library the next day, she noticed the skater boy on a bench just outside, watching her. She froze for just a moment, then tried to hurry away. It was too late; he was already within earshot and calling out to her.

"Do I know you?" he asked.

Basia had no idea how to respond. She didn't recognize him.

"I'm sorry if I freaked you out, it's just that I swear I've seen you somewhere before," he said.

"I don't think so," Basia stammered, her social anxiety kicking into high gear. She might have had a chance at coping with human interaction if she wasn't under so much other stress and fear for her life.

"No, I guess we haven't met, but I still think I've seen you somewhere before. A while ago. I don't know why it's bothering me so much."

This was when Basia had to sit down, her knees were shaking so badly.

"Are you okay?" The boy gripped her arm to help her ease down onto the bench.

Basia just shook her head, taking slow, deep breaths until

she felt she could safely form words again. "Anxiety."

"Is there anything I can do?"

"Aside from stop talking to me, no." Basia realized how rude that sounded as he stepped back a few feet. "I mean, don't go away. I just don't deal with strangers well. Especially lately." Why did she say that last part?

"Why lately?" This boy was awfully nosy.

Basia just shook her head. "So what's your name?"

"Alex." He watched Basia as if she would shatter at any moment.

She wasn't certain that she wouldn't.

"Talk to me. Tell me mundane stuff about yourself. Maybe it will help me calm down." She paused. "And please sit down, you're making me even more nervous hovering over me."

He sat back down on the bench. "Well, I'm a junior technically, though I've been here five years. I've changed my major three times. Right now I'm studying archaeology. Before that it was psychology, but I got bored with that. I've studied it on my own pretty much my entire life anyway. I went in as a journalism student. I made it a full two years there. If I last this semester, I'll tie that for my longest held major. I may even graduate with an archaeology degree. I really enjoy it."

Basia felt her heart slowing down a little, and she could breathe just a bit easier. "What are you going to do when you graduate?"

"I have no idea. I'm really good with computers. I guess maybe I'll get some kind of tech job and squirrel away a bunch of money so I can afford to travel. I could probably get a job with a security company...you know, the people they hire to hack into their systems so they see where the vulnerabilities lie? I'm pretty good at that type of thing. So good that I've never been caught."

Basia stared him in the eye, something she rarely did with anyone, much less a stranger. But she wanted to figure out if he was telling the truth. If he was, maybe he could help her.

He stared right back. "You don't believe me?"

"I don't know. Should I?" Still, Basia didn't break eye contact.

"Believe what you want, it doesn't bother me either way. I know what I can do. I just don't know what I'm going to do with my life."

"Join the club," Basia mumbled, looking away.

"Stuck between majors?" he asked, pushing a lock of hair out of his eyes only for it to immediately fall back to its original position.

"Something like that." Maybe asking Alex about himself hadn't been a good idea. She didn't want to reciprocate with information about herself.

"You haven't told me your name," Alex said.

Don't tell him.

"Basia."

"Basia," he said softly. "Basia...Basia...I know I've seen you somewhere before." His brow furrowed. "That's it! Holy shit, I had no idea..."

"What?" Basia's heart started to race again. She had a feeling she wasn't going to like what Alex was about to tell her.

You shouldn't have told him your name.

"You're the girl that went missing last year. I didn't know they had found you."

"Yeah, well, here I am." This wasn't good. She couldn't afford for anyone else to know who and where she was. "So you saw my picture in the paper, now you know where you've seen me."

"No, that isn't it. There was no picture in the paper. It was just a tiny mention, something about your boss reporting you missing, but no family or anything." He stared at the ground, opened his mouth, then closed it again.

"What?" Basia waited but still he said nothing. "What aren't you telling me?"

"I saw it happen," he said so softly she thought she misheard him.

"You what?"

"I saw you being taken." He continued staring at the ground.

"And you didn't do anything?" Basia clenched her fists at her sides.

Alex finally looked up at her. "Look at me. Do I really look like a guy who could take on two big MMA-looking dudes? I didn't stand a chance. I did go to the police though."

"And?" Basia asked, even though she thought she knew the answer.

"And they took my statement and said they'd call me if they needed anything, but I never heard from them. I got the feeling they wanted to sweep the whole thing under the rug for some reason."

"Shit." Basia slumped on the bench. This was worse than she'd thought. "Where did it happen?"

"I was skating down Woodrail when I heard you shout out from the alley behind an apartment building. I went to see what was going on, but when I saw those guys, I knew I couldn't do anything. Do you know how bad it sucks being so helpless?"

"Yeah, actually, I do," Basia said in an angrier tone than she intended. Woodrail was the street she'd lived on.

"Sorry, I guess you do." Alex hung his head.

They sat in silence for a few minutes, then Alex stood up. She expected him to say goodbye and leave her to go her own way. "Come on, let's go get something to eat."

May as well now that he knows who you are.

"I don't have any-"

"I'm buying. Don't argue. Let's go." He walked away, not looking back to see if she would follow.

Alex drove to Broadway Diner in a faded-blue 1995 Chevy Cavalier. Basia ordered the deluxe breakfast. She felt a little guilty letting some guy she'd just met pay, but her stomach didn't allow her to argue. It was the best meal she'd had since - well, she didn't know when. The last decent meal she remembered had been even before the last night at the restaurant. That night she'd been too anxious to eat.

"Get some more if you want, I don't mind. I make decent money doing freelance web design. Already squirreling away for my travels, I suppose."

Basia declined with a shake of her head.

"Suit yourself. So where are you staying? I'll give you a ride back."

Basia stopped with her fork halfway to her mouth, scrambled eggs falling back to the plate.

"Don't tell me you don't have a place to stay?" Alex said, eyebrows raised.

"Um..."

"Well, I know you don't know me, but you can stay with me if you want. I live alone, you can have the couch for as long as you need. Maybe help me clean up a bit in return. Cleaning isn't my strong suit."

"I couldn't," Basia started, but didn't know what else to say. It would be nice to have a warm, safe place to sleep. But would it be safe? Alex was right, she didn't know him. She felt as if she could trust him, and she didn't trust easily. He didn't know the cops were looking for her, so he really had no reason to call them and report her. But he was smart. He could figure out her situation with a few keystrokes.

"I'm not going to report you to anyone. I don't know what kind of trouble you're in, but it's obvious something is wrong. I don't care about that. Hey, I told you I'm a hacker. I mind my own business, but I like to help people when I can. I won't push you, but if you change your mind, you can find me in the student union." He walked to the register with the receipt. He didn't stare Basia down or pressure her in any way. Just left her at the table to make her decision.

Go.

Just that one word was all Basia needed to decide to take a chance with him. She supposed at some point she'd have to trust someone, and she really did hope he could help her find out more information. If she decided to open up to him, that was.

Decision made, she followed him to the register. "Thanks. I really appreciate it. Your apartment will be spotless," she smiled for the first time in as long as she could remember.

He smiled back, and she felt a stirring of something more inside, but immediately shook it away.

CHAPTER 8

"OH MY!" BASIA SCRUNCHED UP her nose when Alex opened the door to his apartment, trying to ward off the stench. "You weren't kidding about the cleaning thing."

"Yeah, sorry, I know it's kind of gross. I should have warned you."

"Open up some windows, then take me to the convenience store to get some cleaning supplies. I'm going to take a wild guess that you don't have any here?" She didn't even feel bad bossing him around like that. She really had her cleaning work cut out for her. "And do you have any incense? It will at least cover the smell until I get this place cleaned up for you."

"I think so, let me look." Alex disappeared around the corner and she heard a closet door open, and shortly thereafter a crash of things falling. "Found some!" he called out.

"Great. Light it up then let's get out of here. How do you live like this?"

Alex only shrugged in reply.

At the store, Basia loaded up with every type of cleaning item she could think of, including a few cheap toothbrushes for cleaning the bathroom. One thing that helped her manage her anxiety was keeping a meticulously clean living space, so she didn't care if Alex made fun of her for cleaning the grout between the bathroom tiles with a toothbrush. He'd thank her when she was done.

Back at his apartment, she shooed him back into his room so she could clean in peace. Cleaning had always calmed her, so after two weeks of fear and turmoil she was finally in her element. This was something she could devote every muscle in her body to, and was the one way she could shut her brain off, and just be calm for a while.

Basia stopped cleaning when Alex called her name. The confused and wary look on his face frightened her. He held out his cell phone to her. "It's for you."

"Very funny. That's not possible, and you know it."

"I do, but it's true anyway."

"Who is it?" she asked as the rag she'd been scrubbing with fell from her hand to the floor.

"He says his name is Dr. Godfrey."

Basia collapsed to her knees and shook her head. "No, it can't be."

"I don't think she wants to talk to you," Alex said into the phone. A moment later, he handed her the phone anyway, all color drained from his face.

She took it from him, her body on autopilot, not understanding how this had happened. She held it to her ear but said nothing.

"Basia dear? Are you there?"

"How did you find me?" she whispered.

"That was easy. My colleague, Dr. Schultz, has been watching you for a very long time. He's always known where you are."

"How long?"

"Since I moved to California. Someone had to keep an eye on you."

"You bastard," she hissed.

"My mother was married when she gave birth to me. My older brother, however, is another story. One that is none of your business. So, how about we get together, it's been a long time. Too long."

"Not long enough," Basia replied, still kneeling on the floor.

"Meet me at Dr. Schultz's office in an hour. Alex can drop you off, but make sure he leaves. He's already proven once how useless he is in protecting you, so it won't do any good."

"How do you know about that?"

"I know far more than you realize," Dr. Godfrey said.

"Are you going to lock me up again?"

"No, I just want to talk to you, to find out how you are."

Don't believe him.

That was one thing she didn't need a mysterious voice to tell her. "What if I don't show up?"

"It will be better for you, and Alex, if you do. You know I can find you now, so it's useless trying to hide." He gave her the address then hung up.

Basia dropped the phone and started crying. She knew he was right; he'd find her no matter what. Even though she had a bad feeling about going to see him, she knew she had to. She had to protect Alex. He had no part in this.

Alex sat on the floor next to her and rested a hand on her shoulder, as if afraid of what she'd do at his touch. She leaned into him and sobbed while he held her. "You don't have to go," he said.

"Yes I do. He'll find me if I don't, so I may as well get it over with. Besides, I have a lot of questions for him." She wiped her nose on her sleeve. "And when you drop me off you have to leave. Don't wait for me. I'm afraid of what he'll do to you if you try to stay. Please do that much for me."

"What he'll do to me? What about what he'll do to you? What has he already done to you Basia?"

She gave him the five-minute version of Dr. Godfrey marrying her mother when she was ten, her mother's illness and eventual death, her suspicions that he killed her, and waking up in the insane asylum.

"I can't leave you alone with him."

"You have to. It's the only chance I have of getting any answers. Anyway, I'll need you to be safe in case anything does happen to me. I don't have anyone."

"I don't like it."

"I don't either, but please promise me you'll leave once you drop me off. I'll find a way to call you when I need a ride back."

Alex stared into her eyes for what seemed like eternity. "All right, I promise. But I'm going to start digging into this guy and see what skeletons he has in his virtual closet."

"Why do you care so much? You just met me," Basia asked.

"You're different from most girls."

Basia laughed once. That was an understatement.

"Not your life, I mean, but you, as a person. I can just tell. You seem like a good, kind person."

"You're not doing this out of some sense of obligation because you couldn't help me when I was kidnapped, are you?"

"Maybe partly, but it's not just that. I like you, is all."

Basia studied his face, looking for some trick, but sensed nothing but sincerity. She pulled her file from the asylum and the handwritten notes she'd taken from the plastic bag she kept them in and gave them to Alex. "Here's what I have already. Please...don't read the file unless something happens to me. It's really personal. He kept notes on me from the moment he married my mother. Promise?"

"I promise," Alex said.

"Okay, let's go get this over with."

They drove in a silence so thick Basia felt as if she couldn't breathe. When Alex parked in the small parking lot of the office building, with Dr. Leon Schultz as the only name on the sign, they sat in silence for a few minutes. Basia knew she had to get out of the car, knew delaying it would do no good, but delayed anyway.

"Well, I guess I'll see you later," she said finally and opened the door.

Alex grabbed her arm and pulled her back in. When she turned to question him, he pulled her to him and kissed her full on the lips, holding her as close as the car would allow him to.

He had no way of knowing Basia's aversion to intimacy. For a moment she froze, then kissed him back, wishing the gear shift wasn't stuck uncomfortably between them.

Finally, Alex pulled away. "Promise you'll come back to me."

"I'll try," Basia said, not wanting to make a promise she might not be able to keep.

Weak from fear and Alex's unexpected kiss, Basia walked toward the office. She turned before opening the door to make sure Alex was driving away down, then entered, prepared to fight. "Hello?" she called out. No one was in the waiting room, so she walked down the hallway to the patient rooms. She turned to encounter a mist of something liquid being sprayed in her face.

"Hello, Basia," a man she didn't recognize said before she lost consciousness.

CHAPTER 9

WHEN BASIA WOKE, SHE WAS disoriented. It didn't take long for her to realize she was once again restrained to a hospital bed. She screamed and kicked - at least her legs were free this time, but her arms were strapped out away from her body. She continued screaming until Dr. Godfrey entered the room.

"No one is going to hear you, so you might as well save your voice," he said.

Her screams quieted to a whimper. She remembered the last time she'd seen him. She hadn't been restrained then, but what he'd done had still been terrible. He could only do worse now that she was unable to fight back.

"I think you had some questions for me. So ask." Dr. Godfrey turned and took something out of a drawer.

Basia's whimpers grew louder when she saw the scalpel in his hand.

"Ask," he commanded.

"Why was I locked up in a shut down insane asylum?"

Because you're crazy.

"For experiments, of course. You always did fascinate me, if you remember."

"What did you do to me in there?"

"I wanted to see what would happen to someone cursed with anxiety who was left alone in a supposedly haunted asylum for an extended period of time. We tried sensory deprivation experiments, alternated those with sensory overload, be it imagery or noise or light. We piped in noises to terrify you. Gave you false hope of escape. I'm surprised you didn't break. You were always so close to completely losing your mind, I didn't think you'd last a week. But when a year had gone by, I knew we had to raise the stakes. So we gave you a drug to erase your memory of the last year, then let you wake up and waited to see what you would do."

"What if I hadn't found the way out?" Basia felt a tear run down her cheek. No, she mustn't cry. She knew what happened when she cried.

Why would you ask that? You know he doesn't care whether you live or die.

"Well, it would have been a disappointing end to the experiment then, wouldn't it?"

"You're even more disgusting than I thought." Basia spat at him.

"You always were such a sweet talker. But there, there, dearest, don't cry." Dr. Godfrey stroked her hair and kissed her tears away, starting from just beneath her eye down to her jaw line, then lower where the tears hadn't fallen. She knew what was coming next and tried to retreat into her mind, away from the horror.

He slapped her. "You will stay with me. Don't you dare try to escape."

She couldn't survive this again. She had to at least go away in her head.

"I don't have all my wonderful toys here, so I'll have to make do with this." He slowly moved the scalpel back and forth in front of Basia's face. "Stay with me and I'll go easy on you."

"No," she whimpered and tried again to hide, only to be rewarded with a slap so hard she swore she felt her brain rattle in her skull.

"You know I like it messy, so if that's what you want, I'm more than happy to oblige." He lightly traced the knife down her arm, creating a thin red line that didn't quite bleed; it could have been nothing more than a bad scratch.

Next he cut her sweatshirt down the middle, lingering between her breasts, his breath hot against her skin. She sobbed, unable to stop herself as he pulled her sweatpants off and continued his path down her body. "You always were a filthy whore," he said when he put his hand between her legs.

"You made me into a whore. You and all your friends."

"And you loved every moment of it. You and your mother both. It's too bad she loved you more than me. Otherwise I wouldn't have had to kill her to prevent her from going to the police, and I'd still have both of you to fuck every night."

Basia tried to kick him while he wasn't looking but missed. *You're so helpless.*

"Come now, bitch, you think that's going to scare me off? Dr. Schultz, I need a bit of assistance." The doctor Basia saw through the haze before she passed out entered the room. "Tie her legs down, please. Then you can help me with her."

Basia closed her eyes and cried while the two doctors, men who were sworn to protect life, took turns with her until she passed out from pain and exhaustion.

Basia was no longer restrained when she woke the next morning. She was bruised and sticky and wanted a hot shower with a Brillo Pad to scrub the doctors' filth off her skin. She settled for cleaning herself up with rough paper towels in the tiny sink.

Dr. Godfrey walked into the room and tossed a bundle of clothes at her. "If you try anything stupid, you will regret it for the rest of your short life." He stood and stared at her.

"Can I have a little privacy?"

"No. You can do whatever you need to do right here while I watch."

"I hate you."

"But I take so much pleasure from you," he said while staring at her naked body. "Now we can have our little chat,"

Dr. Godfrey said when she was dressed. "What do you want to know?"

"How someone as disgusting and twisted as you could have gotten his medical license. And how no one has turned you into the authorities yet."

"I'm very careful in who I trust with my experiments. Our network is very tight-knit. No one person knows every detail about what we do, so we are all essential. No one of us would turn any of the others in, for the experiments would fall apart."

"So Dr. Schultz is helping you?" Basia asked, already knowing the answer.

Dr. Godfrey nodded.

"What are these experiments for?"

"If I told you it wouldn't be as fun. No, I think I'll make you squirm some more before letting you know your purpose. So now you know that I can still get to you as easily as ever. It's quite amusing how you thought you were safe from me these past four years. Since now you know you will never be safe from me, I trust you will go about your life without trying to tell the authorities about any of this."

"And what if I do?"

"Just remember last night. I still have friends with exotic tastes, and you have grown even more beautiful. I could quit medicine altogether and make a very comfortable living from you."

Bile rose in Basia's throat. When the nausea passed, she looked around the room for something she could use as a weapon. She finally caught the glint of the scalpel Dr. Godfrey had used the night before and left on the counter.

"Now, dear, you understand your situation, don't you?" he asked.

Basia dove across the small room for the scalpel then lunged at Dr. Godfrey's throat, missing and slicing his shoulder instead.

"Put the weapon down!" a new voice called out.

Basia looked to see two police officers with their guns drawn, standing at the entrance to the room. She immediately dropped the scalpel and held her hands up. "Please, don't shoot," she cried.

"Get on your knees and keep your hands on your head," the officer said.

She did as they demanded, sobbing the entire time. She knew what this meant. They'd arrest her for assault, and she'd surely be sent to prison with a quick trial. She didn't want to tell them about the rape, knowing Dr. Godfrey had enough influence that they'd believe him over her anyway, yet knew it was her only hope of not being charged with assault. "He raped me, I was only trying to protect myself."

"We know Dr. Godfrey, he's not that type of man. Besides, how could he have raped you when you're fully dressed?" one of the officers asked.

"It was last night," Basia said.

"Then why are you still here?" the other officer asked while putting handcuffs on her.

"I passed out. When I woke up and saw him I thought he was going to do it again."

"Sure, and there just happened to be a scalpel handy for you to attack him with. Why didn't you just leave?"

"I'm not lying! Can't you test me to see that I'm telling the truth?"

"You got money to pay for it?"

"What?" Basia thought she'd misheard the officer.

"If you want a rape kit administered, you'll have to pay for it." He jerked her up to her feet and pushed her toward the door.

"But I don't have any money." Basia cried harder.

"Don't have money, or don't want us to find out you're lying?"

Basia didn't know what else to say as the officer shoved her into the back of the squad car.

He's finally ruined you completely.

As the squad car drove away from Dr. Schultz's office with Basia handcuffed in the back, she saw a blue Nova parked across the street a block away. She knew then that Alex had been the one who called the police.

CHAPTER 10

THE NEXT DAY ALEX VISITED Basia in jail. She finally told him the whole story of her history with Dr. Godfrey and what had happened at Dr. Schultz's office.

"I could bail you out. I have some money saved up and it's kind of just sitting there," he said.

"Don't you dare. You barely know me. Besides, it's safer for me in here where Dr. Godfrey can't get to me. Honestly, as fucked up as it sounds, I'd rather be here until this is all sorted out."

"But-"

"No. Absolutely not." Basia tried hard to stay strong and not cry but felt tears beginning to prick her eyes.

"So what's going to happen now?" Alex asked.

"I don't know. As much influence as Dr. Godfrey has, I can't imagine that they'll just let me go. I guess I'll end up serving some time."

"You could get a lawyer."

"They've already given me one, but I don't have much faith in a state-appointed attorney against someone with as much power as Dr. Godfrey. I lost control, and now I'll have to pay the consequences. Believe me, this is better than what I

48

went through as a child with him. Or the other night." Basia paused. "Anyway, you should probably stay away from me for a while. Don't come visit me."

"But you're all alone."

"Please, Alex, I couldn't stand it if something happened to you because of me. Promise me."

Alex stared at her but said nothing.

"Promise me. Please."

He let out a breath, and his shoulders slumped. "Okay, I promise."

"Thank you. You should probably go now."

Alex stood up and started to walk away, then stopped and turned around. He stared at Basia, eyes sparkling with tears. He walked back to her, pulled her to her feet, and kissed her.

Basia pulled away after a moment. "Why did you do that?"

"Why? I like you, that's why."

"It just puts you in more danger if Dr. Godfrey knows how much you care about me. And anyway, I'm not exactly comfortable with other people touching me."

"Oh god, I'm sorry, I didn't think."

"No, it's okay, I actually don't mind it from you. I'm just on edge right now. I've never had a lot of friends, never dated. I don't know how to take it."

"I understand." They stood staring at the ground. "Well, I guess I'll go now."

"Yeah, I guess so." Basia knew it was safer for him to stay away, but her heart already ached with longing.

"Can I kiss you once more before I leave?" Alex asked.

Basia nodded, wondering if this was how normal high school kids felt on first dates. He held her tight and kissed her, then turned and walked away without another word.

Basia saw the flowers bloom, and then wilt form the heat of summer through the bars of the recreation field at the jail where she was held. She went through meetings with more state psychiatrists than she could count in those two months of limbo, wondering which ones knew Dr. Godfrey, yet knowing she could never ask. Of course, they wouldn't be publicly affiliated with him. That would lead to an unfair assessment. In early July, she was declared mentally incapable of standing trial, and was sent to a state run mental hospital. When she was told the ruling, she suffered a panic attack and had to be heavily sedated. She could only imagine what sort of access Dr. Godfrey would have to her on his own turf.

When she dragged herself out of the haze of sedation, she found she had already been transferred to the hospital. She woke in a sterile white room with one bed and was grateful that she was not restrained. She wasn't sure her sanity could handle waking up to that again, though she was sick of waking up in unfamiliar, institutional places. What had her life become? It hadn't been much before, but at least she'd had the shell of an existence. Now she had nothing.

Maybe this is what you were meant for, the voice said, and this time sounded as if it came from outside her head, even though there was clearly no one around.

Basia walked to the door and found that she was locked in. Five minutes of knocking finally brought a nurse. The nurse paused at the door and eyed Basia. What had she done to be regarded in that manner? She went back to sit on the bed, hands folded in her lap, hoping she presented herself as harmless so the nurse would come talk to her.

"I'm not going to hurt anyone," Basia said when the nurse finally unlocked the door.

The nurse didn't respond. "I'll get you some water then have the doctor come talk to you."

The last thing Basia wanted was to see another doctor, but she knew she had no choice. "Please, I don't want to see Dr. Schultz," Basia said when the nurse came back.

"I don't know who that is," the nurse said as she left the room.

A while later, a doctor Basia didn't recognize greeted her. "Hello, Basia. I'm Dr. Thomas Ridgeway, but you can call me Dr. Tom. How are you?"

Basia almost laughed. "I've been better."

"The nurse told me you begged not to see a Dr. Schultz. Who is he, and why don't you want to see him?"

Basia knew she couldn't say anything about the rape and realized she shouldn't have even mentioned his name. She knew Dr. Godfrey would somehow have access to her files here, and he'd be very upset at that breach of confidentiality. But Basia was disoriented from the sedative and exhaustion. "I don't know, I don't know what I'm saying, I'm just confused and tired." She hoped this doctor wouldn't make a note of the name in her file. If he was a good doctor, he would, and would try to find out who it was. She hoped he wasn't that good. As soon as she thought that she giggled, realizing how absurd it was to hope to have a doctor who wasn't good at his job.

You're never going to get out of here acting like that.

"What's so funny, Basia? Can you share?" Dr. Tom asked.

"I'm just so tired. I shouldn't be here, I'm not going to hurt anyone."

"We can talk about that later. I don't want to wear you out anymore right now. I just wanted to stop in and introduce myself when the nurse told me you were awake. Get some rest now. I'll talk to you more tomorrow."

Basia stayed in her room as much as possible, and when forced out into the common area, she sat in a chair in a corner, trying to remain invisible so the other patients would leave her alone. She saw some of them have visits from friends and family. Occasionally, she would hope for a visit from Alex, but was ultimately grateful that he kept his promise.

He's probably forgotten about you. He just wanted to be able to tell his buddies he kissed a crazy girl and made her think he cared.

No, he remembered her from the night she was kidnapped. He remembered the tiny blurb in the paper about her going missing. He wouldn't have forgotten about her, though Basia knew it was safer for him if he had. And no matter how hard she tried, she couldn't forget his kiss. The softness of his lips was electrifying. She'd never known physical intimacy could be gentle and caring. She wished she had some chance at a relationship with him, but didn't dare hope for such an outrageous dream.

Basia hadn't seen or heard from Dr. Godfrey since she'd been committed, but she knew that didn't mean he was leaving her alone. She was certain he had access to Dr. Tom's notes, and was always careful not to talk of him or her childhood in her therapy sessions.

"Basia, I know you don't want to be here forever," Dr. Tom said. "But if you're ever going have a chance at freedom, you're going to have to open up to me so we can make some progress. I don't even know what caused your transgression, much less how to help you work through your issues."

Transgression. Issues. These were words Basia had grown to despise thanks to Dr. Tom. Her transgression was an attempt at freedom. One that backfired horribly. But how could she tell him that?

"I don't know what came over me. I don't even remember doing that," she said for what felt like the thousandth time.

Dr. Tom sighed, frustrated at reaching the end of another unproductive therapy session with Basia. "Please try to think about it. I truly want to help you, but you have to work with me."

Basia stood and left without another word.

She bumped into another patient as she walked down the hallway lost in thought. "Oh, I'm sorry."

"You're Dr. Godfrey's stepdaughter, aren't you?" the girl said.

Basia's heart raced. "I don't know-who? What are you talking about?"

"You know who I mean. Quick, come in here." The girl pulled Basia into an empty room. "I see it in your eyes. He locked me up too, years ago. I was transferred here when the hospital in Kirksville closed. I haven't had any encounters with him in years."

Basia simply stared at this girl, unsure what to say, what was safe to say. How could she know who Basia was? Was she a plant, some part of Dr. Godfrey's sinister plan?

"You don't trust me. I understand. I wouldn't trust me either. But ask around. You'll find out I've been here for five years. You'll find out I'm not a plant, that I'm real. But I'm not crazy. As hard as he tried, he couldn't break me." Footsteps echoed down the hall. "Quick, hide behind the door!" The girl pulled Basia out of sight as a nurse walked by. "I'm Jocelyn Ackerman," she said when the nurse had passed. "I'll see you around." She darted out of the room, leaving Basia slightly dazed and very confused.

Basia didn't know what to think of Jocelyn. She asked a few patients about her, and found out that she had, in fact, been there for five years. That didn't mean she still wasn't somehow working for Dr. Godfrey. But the girl seemed genuine.

A week later, Basia saw Jocelyn in the common room. Jocelyn said nothing, only waved, giving Basia her space. After a few more encounters like this, Basia decided to talk to the girl again. No warning bells went off in Basia's head. Besides, what could it hurt? She was starting to feel safe from Dr. Godfrey in this place.

Talk to her. She can help you.

Basia sat on a couch that was backed up to the one on which Jocelyn sat. "What do you know about Dr. Godfrey?" she asked.

"He's sick. I went to see a school doctor when I started suffering from depression. It was just homesickness and stress, really, but it got worse when my parents were killed in a car accident. They're they only family I had." Jocelyn turned to look Basia in the eye. "I was completely alone after that. I didn't have any friends in school. You were alone too, weren't you?"

Basia nodded.

"Thought so. When my depression got worse, the school doctor sent me to Dr. Schultz, who somehow determined that I was a danger to myself, even though I'd never shown any signs of being suicidal. He got me committed to Kirksville Manor. It was a very small hospital and didn't get the funding it needed. That's why it closed. But before it did, Dr. Godfrey did terrible things to me. He flew in periodically for the experiments. Sensory deprivation experiments, sensory overload experiments, experimental drugs...and other things."

"What other things?"

"He thought he could fuck my depression away. When he couldn't, he let his sicko friends try."

Basia felt sick to her stomach. Because she had run away and hidden from Dr. Godfrey, this poor girl had been subjected to the same treatment. "I'm so sorry."

"Not your fault."

"Yeah, it kind of is. I ran away from home, so he didn't have me anymore. Guess he found someone else."

"Still not your fault. I wonder if he's forgotten about me. He's so methodical, it seems unlikely, but I can't imagine he'd knowingly risk you meeting me."

"Unless that's part of his plan to screw with our heads," Basia said. She saw Dr. Tom walking through the common room just then. "I have to go," she said and hurried to the other side of the room, hoping he hadn't seen her talking to Jocelyn. If what Jocelyn said was true, she didn't want their association to be documented.

That night, Basia lay awake in bed, unable to sleep, Jocelyn's story running through her head. If she were telling the truth, Basia had to get out of there, had to find a way to get free and expose Dr. Godfrey. How many other girls had suffered because of him? There was no way to know, unless she could somehow find his personal files. She knew he kept detailed notes on everything - her own file had proven that. Somehow, she had to get out and get access to them. Even if it meant flying to California and breaking into his house.

But first she'd have to figure out how to work with Dr. Tom without giving away anything about Dr. Godfrey. She'd have to concoct a believable story about why she would have attacked him without letting on that he had raped her and pimped her out to his friends before she even hit puberty. She read enough news stories to know that he wouldn't get more than a few years in prison from those crimes, and then he'd come after her with an even stronger vengeance. No, she had to find a way to get him out of the picture for good.

She was going to have to ask Alex to help her once she regained her freedom. She didn't like him being any more involved than he already was, but she had no choice. For better or worse, she trusted him, and he already knew her story anyway.

CHAPTER 11

BASIA WORKED HARD AT CONVINCING Dr. Tom she could be "cured" and given her freedom again. She concocted a story about a young girl distraught at losing her father; a girl who hated Dr. Godfrey for trying to take his place. When she lost her mother as well to a mysterious, incurable disease, she resented being left in the care of a man she had never forgiven for replacing her father. Because she had a legitimate history of severe anxiety, and with the ordeal of her being missing for a year - she continued to claim she didn't remember anything after her walk home from work that night - she had a fairly easy time of convincing him the stress was just too much for her when she finally saw the man she hated again.

"Why did you agree to meet with him, if you dislike him so strongly?" Dr. Tom asked.

"I didn't know what to do. I wasn't thinking clearly," Basia said, fists clenched.

"Calm down, Basia, I believe you, I'm just trying to understand why you were thinking the way you were so I can best help you."

"Sorry," she said, looking down into her lap. Getting angry certainly was not the way to convince him she should be let free.

"We can stop for today if you're tired."

"No, I want to work through this. I'll be fine."

"If you're certain..."

Basia nodded.

"Okay, so after you called him, what happened?"

Don't screw this up, or you'll end up here forever.

Basia had planned this out in her head, hoping Dr. Godfrey hadn't told something completely different to the cops. "He said he'd flown in from California to help me, and for me to meet him at his colleague's office. I didn't want to see him, but I didn't think I had any other choice. I had nothing and I was scared." Part of that was true anyway.

"So you met him at the office, then what?" Dr. Tom looked up from his notes to ask.

"I don't exactly remember. We were talking, and things got heated. I think he said something about my mom, but I don't remember what, and that's when I lost it. I guess the reminder that I've lost everything in my life was just too much for me to handle under such a stressful situation."

"That's understandable. I'm sure you've suffered quite an awful ordeal, even if you don't remember what happened yet. Anyone could act out of character in such circumstances. I'd like to help you work through your anger against Dr. Godfrey."

"I'd like that," Basia lied. She didn't want to let go of her anger. It was the one thing she had left. But she knew she'd have to fake it if she were ever going to get out and help Jocelyn, not to mention somehow stopping Dr. Godfrey from hurting any other girls.

"When you first went to the police station, you said something about Dr. Godfrey having done horrible things to you. What did you mean by that?"

Basia hadn't taken into consideration that Dr. Tom might know about that. "I don't remember saying that," she trailed off.

"It's all right, we can talk about that later. I think we've discussed enough for today anyway. Try to get some rest."

Basia tried to limit her interaction with Jocelyn so as not to set off any red flags with Dr. Godfrey if he was monitoring them. She explained why, thankful that Jocelyn understood. She also made good progress with Dr. Tom. She was able to write off her comment about Dr. Godfrey to the police as something a confused girl said. In late November, Dr. Tom presented his case for releasing her to the oversight committee. Basia spent the entire week before terrified that she would be released and that she wouldn't be. If she were, it would mean Dr. Godfrey had easy access to her again. If she weren't, it meant, well, it was obvious what that meant.

She also missed Alex and was scared he wouldn't want to see her again after six months of being locked away in a mental institute for criminals.

On the day of Dr. Tom's meeting with the committee, Basia paced circles around the common room for hours until a nurse called her into his office. She continued to pace a smaller circle in his office while waiting for him to arrive.

"Basia, please sit," he said.

She did, legs bouncing up and down.

"I have good news. The committee agrees with me that you are ready to be released."

Basia said nothing. She felt numb, not having known which answer would be worse.

"Aren't you happy?"

"Yes, I'm just shocked. I mean, I didn't know what to expect. And I guess I'm a little scared too. Where will I go? What will I do?"

How will you avoid being used by Dr. Godfrey again?

"You'll work with an occupational therapist. We'll set you up with a place to stay and help you find a job. You won't be alone."

Of course you won't. Dr. Godfrey will be waiting for you.

Basia nodded, trying to absorb everything Dr. Tom said and ignore the voice in her head at the same time.

"You'll have therapy sessions twice a week and will meet with me once a week in my office outside of the hospital. After a month of that schedule, you and I will meet every other week, and it will go down from there until eventually you're down to only one therapy session every two weeks. But that will take time. I'm sure you'll do fine, Basia. You've made wonderful progress here, and I'm delighted I was able to help you."

"Thank you, Dr. Tom, I really appreciate it," she said softly, overwhelmed by all the information.

When Basia left the office, she couldn't help but want to tell Jocelyn the good news. She found the girl and motioned at her to follow her into an empty room where no one would notice their conversation.

"That's wonderful!" Jocelyn exclaimed a little too loudly for Basia's comfort.

"I know, but I'm really scared too. What if Dr. Godfrey gets to me again once I'm out?"

"You'll just have to be careful. Don't be alone in secluded places."

"I'd better go. Dr. Tom hasn't said anything to me about our friendship, so I hope he hasn't noticed and made any notes about it. I'm sure Dr. Godfrey is somehow getting access to his notes, and I don't want him to know I have more proof against him, much less to be reminded that you're here." Basia checked the hallway to make sure no one was in sight, then went back to the common room to her usual chair in the corner, avoiding contact with everyone.

Basia was released from Columbia Behavioral Hospital a week later, during the bitter January cold. The social worker drove her to a group home where she'd be able to stay until she could afford a place of her own. She'd gotten a job on the night cleaning crew at an office building. She was thankful it was a job that didn't require much interaction with people, only the others who cleaned the building, and as she found out, they weren't talkative either. Of course, they were also Russian immigrants who spoke little English, so that may have contributed to their introverted behavior.

Basia welcomed the cleaning job, as it helped her to stay calm. It wasn't ideal that it was at night though, as she was scared out of her wits walking home alone. She got into the habit of taking a Xanax every night a half hour before she had to leave, just so she could survive the walk and stave off the panic attack until she made it back to the group home. Then, when she finally made it back safely and went to sleep, she had horrible nightmares every night.

It's only a matter of time before he gets to you, the voice kept telling her.

After a week of this, she could stand it no longer. She broke down and called Alex, having memorized his number before going to meet Dr. Godfrey all those months ago. She smiled at the sound of his voice, but didn't immediately reply when he answered, scared of how he'd react to hearing from her.

"Hello? Is someone there?" A pause. "Okay, I'm hanging up now."

"Alex!" Basia finally blurted out, knowing she wouldn't be able to dial his number again if he hung up.

"Basia? Is that you?"

"Yes." She almost expected him to hang up anyway, knowing it was her. His response took her by surprise.

"I'm so relieved to hear from you. I've been so worried. I've tried to keep track of you by hacking into the hospital's computer system. Shit, that sounds kind of creepy. I'm sorry."

"Don't be. It's nice to know you cared." A knot in her stomach untied, and she was finally able to breathe again.

"Can I see you? Is it safe?"

Her heart flip-flopped at the eagerness in his voice. "I doubt it's safe, but I need to see a friendly face." *And to ask you to be my escort every night I work,* she thought, but didn't drop that on him yet.

"Where are you staying? I'll come pick you up."

"It's kind of embarrassing." She twirled her hair around her finger.

"Basia, you don't have to hide anything from me."

She knew if she wanted him to walk her home she'd have to tell him sooner or later, so gave in. "It's a group home. It kind of sucks, but at least it has a bed and heat."

"There's nothing wrong with that. It's better than living on the streets like you were when I first met you. When should I pick you up?"

"Whenever you can." She paused, debating how much vulnerability she wanted to show. "I really need a hug."

"That I can provide. I'll be there in twenty minutes."

Basia wished she had something nicer than the worn out jeans and sweatshirt she'd been given, but then felt silly for wishing that. Alex was probably just feeling sorry for her. He'd likely forgotten all about their kiss and found a nice, sane girl to date. She sighed in resignation, convinced she'd always be alone in the world.

CHAPTER 12

BASIA SAT OUTSIDE IN THE cold night air waiting for Alex to arrive. If she didn't like the idea of him knowing where she lived, she liked the idea of him going inside even less. She knew it wasn't her fault that she lived in such a place, but she still hated it. He was right though; it was better than living on the streets. At least here she had a bed and access to a shower, even if there wasn't always hot water.

She didn't like sharing the space with so many others who had truly been crazy or criminal. She had only been framed. They made her nervous, so much so that she never slept or showered without a knife nearby. That knife had been the first thing she'd bought with her first paycheck. It wasn't great, and probably wouldn't stand up in a real fight. Twenty dollars from a sporting goods store. But it made her feel slightly less vulnerable to the people she wasn't convinced were completely rehabilitated.

She swore to work as hard as she could to get her own place as soon as possible.

Alex pulled up, still driving the faded-blue Chevy Cavalier. Basia planned to just slide into the front seat without fanfare, but he put the car in park, got out, and ran to give her a bear hug. It took her a moment to relax into his embrace, having had no physical contact other than nurses prodding her with needles and blood pressure bands and thermometers since the last time she'd seen him. Once she did though, once she accepted his concern, the tears began, and she couldn't stop them.

"I'm sorry, I thought I'd be all out of tears," she said as Alex led her to sit in his car, which he'd left running with the heat on.

"Don't apologize. You've been through more than most people can even imagine."

As he held her across the console of the car, the tears slowed, then stopped. She hoped it would be the last time she cried for a long time. "Can we go somewhere?"

"Of course. Where do you want to go?"

"I don't care, anywhere but here. I hate it here." She stood, eager to get away from the group home.

"Are you hungry?" Alex asked.

Basia shrugged. She hadn't eaten all day, and hadn't had a truly good meal since Alex had taken her to the diner. "I should probably eat. Just not anywhere too expensive. I don't have a lot of money."

"Nonsense. You probably need a good meal, so I'm going to buy you one," Alex said.

"Really, you don't have to. I can afford food now, just not expensive food."

"I want to. So stop arguing."

"All right," Basia sighed. She really didn't understand why he'd spend money on someone like her, but didn't have the energy to argue.

He took her to a chain Italian restaurant and ordered an appetizer sampler for them to split while waiting for the entrees. She didn't want to talk about anything too serious while eating, so she asked him about school.

"Believe it or not I'm still studying archaeology. Actually I'm going to graduate in May," he said with a smile.

"Good for you. What are you going to do?"

"I have no idea. I haven't really started looking for a job

yet. I guess I'm content here for the time being." He stared at Basia.

"What? Why are you looking at me like that?" she asked, a mozzarella stick halfway to her mouth.

"I didn't want to leave while you were in there," he said.

"Oh. But now you will?"

"I didn't mean it like that."

"Don't you have a girlfriend or something who would try to keep you away from me?"

"No." He picked up a loaded potato skin.

"Oh." Basia didn't know what else to say. "Well you should still do something with your life other than wait for me."

"I am. I'm helping you. You wouldn't believe the dirt I've been able to dig up on Dr. Godfrey. But I still have a long way to go before you'll be able to make a solid case against him."

"Can we not talk about this until after we eat? I'm sure the food is great, and I really don't want to lose my appetite."

"Sure, sorry," Alex said. "I didn't think."

"It's okay, most college students don't have to worry about dealing with mental cases like me."

"You're not a mental case. I wish you'd stop saying such awful things about yourself, Basia. You're a bright girl who's been dealt a shit hand in life. None of what's happened is your fault."

"Is that true though? What if I had told someone what he did to me when I was a kid? Maybe none of this would have happened." Basia stared down at the table.

"You were just a kid, you didn't know any better. You're supposed to be able to trust parental figures. You're going to make me switch back to studying psychology just so I can break you out of this self-destructive way of thinking."

Basia looked up at him. "No! You're about to graduate, you can't do that!"

"I'm kidding, Basia," Alex said. "But seriously. How are you really?"

"I don't know. I mean, I'm glad I'm out, but I have this night job cleaning an office building, and I have to walk home by myself and it terrifies me. I'm so scared..." She couldn't finish the thought, that Dr. Godfrey would take her again. "And some of the people that live with me really scare me too. I wonder how anyone thought they were ready to be released."

"Is there anything I can do to help?"

"Well...could you drive me home a couple nights a week? You don't have to every night I work. I hate to ask because I don't get off until after midnight."

"Done. Tell me your schedule, and I'll be there. Every night. I don't want anything to happen to you."

"Thank you so much, Alex. I really don't understand why you're doing all this for me. I mean, you barely even know me."

"I told you before. I like you. It's as simple as that." He reached across the table for Basia's hand.

They were finished with their meals, and Basia figured it was time to talk about the hard stuff. "So what have you found out about Dr. Godfrey?"

"Back in the 70s he was involved in a lot of really controversial experiments on his mental patients. That wasn't really a shock to me. What was surprising was that he had official funding for the experiments, and patients' families willingly enrolled their loved ones in these experiments. He really had the medical community fooled with what he was doing."

"My god." Basia worried that she might lose her dinner and took a drink of water, willing it to stay down.

"The fucked up thing is, he had everything documented. The experiments were eventually shut down when someone went public with the details, but since they were official, he never suffered any consequences.

The conversation paused, and then Basia remembered she hadn't told Alex about Jocelyn yet. "I have to tell you about Jocelyn, this girl I met in the hospital." Basia told Alex all about her and the experiments Dr. Godfrey had done on her, and how she wanted to help the girl get out.

"So now we have to find solid proof of what he's been doing. I still have the files you gave me and have added Dr. Ridgeway's notes. We need to get into Dr. Godfrey's and Dr.

Schultz's computers and find any notes they might have kept on you in between that time, and anything they might have on Jocelyn or any other girls. We have a lot of work ahead of us. Do you think you can handle this?"

Basia nodded. "I have to. I don't see what other choice I have. I can't let him keep doing these awful things to people."

"If it gets to be too much, promise you'll tell me? Please?"

"I promise. I don't want to end up back there legitimately. It was hard enough convincing them I'm sane when I never was crazy in the first place. If I really lost it, I don't think I'd ever get out."

CHAPTER 13

IT WAS THE END OF February, and Alex was finally able to hack into Dr. Godfrey's and Dr. Schultz's home computers. In that time, Basia had her required therapy visits decreased to once every two weeks. She looked forward to the time when it would be only once a month. Then, she hoped to move away from Columbia, even if it was just to St. Louis. At least she'd be farther away from Dr. Schultz's watchful eye, because she was certain he was still keeping tabs on her for Dr. Godfrey. Of course, as much as she hated to admit it to herself, her moving depended on if Alex would move as well. She was falling for him, and even if he didn't feel the same, she didn't want to leave her only friend.

When Alex finally had the information they needed to present a case against Dr. Godfrey, he insisted they celebrate with dinner at a fancy restaurant. He even ordered a bottle of wine for them to split.

"What are you going to do when this is all over?" Basia asked him, both needing and fearing the answer.

"My counselor from college called me last week. There's an archaeological dig in South America she thinks I'd be great for. She knows the guy heading it up, so she only has to say the word and the job is mine. I've been thinking about maybe putting my degree to use now that I finally have one."

See, just one more person who's going to leave you behind. Why do you even bother getting attached? the voice said.

That was exactly what Basia had feared, but she tried to stay cheerful for Alex's sake. He hadn't kissed her again since she'd regained her freedom, though there had been plenty of hugs and friendly cuddling on the couch while watching movies. Basia hadn't yet moved out of the group home, but was close to having enough money saved up to feel secure venturing out on her own. It didn't much matter, for she spent much of her time at Alex's apartment anyway, sleeping on the couch when she was too tired to go home.

"I don't have to, though. I mean, I'm not sure how I feel about all the immunization shots I'd have to get and still probably catching some awful illness."

"No, you should go. It's a wonderful opportunity." Basia forced a smile onto her face.

"But what about you?"

"I'll be fine, don't worry about me. I might even go back to school myself. As bullshit as my story may have been, my anxiety is actually getting better with all the therapy. Xanax actually works, so I think I could handle school."

"What do you want to study?" Alex took a sip of wine.

"I haven't thought that far. I want to help people. There's no way I could go into psychology or anything like that though. Maybe teaching."

"I think you'd be a wonderful teacher."

Basia laughed, looking down at her plate. "How can you say that? I can barely even look at you when we're talking. How can you think I'd be good standing up in front of a room full of kids?"

Alex reached across the table and lifted Basia's chin so she was forced to look him in the eye. "Because you're kind, and you care. The world needs more teachers with those qualities."

They stared into each other's eyes for a long moment before Basia turned away, forcing Alex to drop his hand from her cheek. She took a long drink of wine, unsure what else to do. Sure, she'd hoped for Alex to be attracted to her, but now that it appeared he was, she didn't know how to react. She also didn't know how much of his attraction was due to the almost empty bottle of wine they'd split.

He just wants to sleep with you.

"It's not the wine, Basia," he said as if reading her mind.

"What?" She tried to act like nothing had happened.

"I've been attracted to you from the moment I saw you in the student union. You're beautiful, and just so...real. Not like all these other college kids who try so hard to be something they're not."

"But you're going to go to South America." She set her wine glass down.

"I didn't say that. I said it was an option, and an interesting one. I guess I wanted to see how you'd react. I have no idea how you feel about me, you're so closed off most of the time."

"I just...I didn't want to ruin anything. You're my only friend, and I don't know what I'd do without you. I mean, even if you went to South America, you'd still be my friend, I just wouldn't be able to see you or talk to you every day. But if I did something stupid and scared you away..."

"You can't scare me away Basia."

"Then why haven't you kissed me again since I got out?" There. She'd said it. As stupid and childish as it sounded, she'd asked.

"I didn't want to overwhelm you. And like I said, I had no idea how you felt about me."

"So why now?"

"Well, I figured maybe since we have what we need against Dr. Godfrey, even though I know it's still going to be a long road, maybe you'd be a little more relaxed and...receptive?"

"Oh, Alex. I wish you would have said something sooner. But promise me something."

"What?"

"Go to South America. I'll still be here when you get back. I don't want you to miss that opportunity because of me. I hate to think of what opportunities you may have already passed up because you've been watching out for me. Promise me that?"

Alex stared into her eyes as if searching for a trick. Finally, he said, "I promise. But I'll miss you every minute I'm there."

"I'll just take a super-heavy course load so I don't have time or energy to miss you," Basia laughed.

Once Alex paid for dinner, they went back to his apartment. Basia stood inside the doorway while he hung their coats. She suddenly felt awkward and unsure of what to do next.

He stood a few feet from her, seeming just as awkward and unsure.

"So what now?" she finally asked.

"What do you want?" Alex asked.

"God, I don't know. I'd never even kissed anyone until you. I have no idea how this is supposed to work." She stared down at the floor. "Only how it's not."

"We don't have to do anything. Just because I told you I'm attracted to you doesn't mean we have to do anything that makes you uncomfortable."

"I don't know what will make me uncomfortable, that's the problem. I bet you wish you hadn't said that now, huh? I'm not exactly the easiest girl to understand."

"I don't care about that, Basia. I care about you. So if you want to just sit on the couch and watch movies, that's fine with me."

"Well, how about we sit on the couch and watch movies then, but maybe you can kiss me while we do?"

"That sounds like a wonderful plan," Alex said.

A half hour into the movie, Basia relaxed enough to move on with the second part of her plan. She and Alex kissed on the couch until the movie was over. She wondered if this was what normal college kids did.

"Do you want to go lie down?" Alex asked when the movie ended. "I mean, just lie down. Nothing else."

"Yeah, I think I'd like that," Basia said, her heart racing. What if she wanted something else? She thought she did, but the remembered she didn't know anything about what sex was supposed to be like. Alex had been slow and gentle so far. She had no reason to believe he'd act otherwise just because they moved to his bedroom.

It didn't take long before Basia pulled Alex's shirt over his head, and he followed her lead. She was surprised how good his caresses felt all over her body. She'd never felt anything so gentle before, and it made her weep.

"I'm sorry, Basia, I didn't mean to go too far, I didn't mean to make you cry," he said, eyes wide.

"No, it's not that. It's just, I've never been touched like that. It's wonderful," she whispered.

"Do you want me to stop?" Alex clearly had no idea how to react to a half-naked girl crying in his bed. It was probably most men's worst nightmare.

"No, please, don't stop. Just hold me for a few minutes, but I don't want you to stop."

"Are you sure?"

Basia only nodded, and kissed him to prove her point. After she'd stopped crying and they kissed some more, Alex straddled her. When he lowered himself toward her body, Basia tensed up, panic threatening to overwhelm her. "Stop, please," she cried, and this time the tears weren't of joy, they were of fear. "I'm sorry, Alex, I thought I could do this," she sobbed into his chest after he pulled the sheet over them.

"Ssshhhh, don't be sorry. I shouldn't have gone so fast. I should have thought. I'm the one who should apologize."

Look at you, screwing everything up again. Way to go.

"Alex, you don't have to apologize because I'm fucked up. Everything was so wonderful up until the end." She sat up, pulling the sheet more firmly around her. "I should go home."

He gently caught her arm. "Is that what you really want?"

Basia was surprised to see his eyes sparkle with unshed tears, which only quickened her own. "No. It's probably what you want though."

"It isn't," he said. "I'd like you to stay, if you want."

"I'd like that." After putting on a pair of Alex's boxers and one of his T-shirts, she curled up next to him in bed and cried herself to sleep while he held her.

CHAPTER 14

THE NEXT MORNING ALEX SAID nothing about the previous night, sensing it was best to let Basia bring it up, or not, as she felt comfortable. Instead, they had breakfast, and then started the hunt for a lawyer who would help them make a case against Dr. Godfrey. They knew it would be hard since he was so well regarded in the medical community, and the allegations were so shocking. Kidnapping, rape, and medical experiments weren't exactly something lawyers likely handled every day.

Basia was surprised that Alex had already researched lawyers and chosen one, Mr. David Templeton, to suggest they go to. "How did you have time for that while also hacking into Dr. Godfrey's computer?"

"Pure talent," he said. "And lots of coffee. It also helps that my job is way too simplistic for me, so I have tons of spare time after getting all my work done."

"I'm impressed. I wouldn't have even known where to begin."

"I just started searching for lawyers who handled medical cases, then narrowed it down from there based on win rate, type of cases handled, that kind of thing."

"And that's why I leave the computer stuff to you."

Alex cleared his throat. "I hope you don't mind that I already set up an appointment with him for this afternoon."

Basia's stomach dropped, and she felt the color drain from her face.

You're going to file a lawsuit against him, and he's going to come for you and do worse things than ever.

"I'm sorry, I should have waited. I just got excited at having what we need and want to see this all over for you. I should have asked you first."

"No, it's not that, it's just...I'm scared what's going to happen to me, what Dr. Godfrey is going to do to me when he finds out what we've done. And I'm even more scared what he's going to do to you when he finds out how much you've helped me. I mean, this is basically all your doing. I didn't do anything except give you the background info."

"I thought this was what you wanted though?"

"It is, it's just scary. Thank you for making the appointment though."

Basia dressed in her best khakis and polo shirt - which weren't all that great, but she hadn't seen the need to spend much on clothing. It was better than jeans and a sweatshirt though, and Alex didn't upstage her, trying to make her more comfortable.

"Mr. Harrington, Miss Reed. A pleasure to meet you. I'm sorry I don't have anything prepared for you, but Mr. Harrington was vague on the details of your case."

"Alex is fine. And it's a very sensitive case," Alex said.

"Every case receives my utmost attention and confidentiality where possible."

"I understand, but I didn't want to bring up the details over the phone. And it's really Basia's story to tell, I'm just helping her out as a friend."

"How can I help you, Basia?"

Basia had taken a Xanax before the meeting, hoping it would stave off any panic attacks, though she felt her chest tighten. "Well, it's a really long and difficult story." She took a deep breath.

"Take your time," Mr. Templeton said.

Yes, take your time, Dr. Godfrey will be waiting for you until the day you die.

Trying to ignore the voice, Basia told him the basics, not going into too much detail just yet, wanting to get it all out as quickly as possible before she lost her nerve. She started with her dad's death and went all the way up to the present, including Dr. Godfrey raping her after she escaped the asylum. She left the details of how they got the files to Alex to explain since it wasn't exactly legal. She was proud of herself for only having to stop to regain her composure once.

"You realize these are very serious allegations? Having worked with medical lawsuits for so long, I've heard Dr. Godfrey's name. I don't know him personally, but I do know he is highly respected. This will be a very difficult case," Mr. Templeton said.

You see, no one will believe you.

"I know, but I can't stand by and do nothing. I'm not the only girl he's done this to." Basia told him about Jocelyn. "He's a terrible person and has to be stopped."

"I'll request a copy of the rape kit that was administered after you were arrested. That will help."

"They didn't do one," Basia said, staring into her lap.

"Excuse me?" Mr. Templeton said.

"The police didn't believe me, and told me I'd have to pay for it myself. I didn't have any money, so they wouldn't do it."

He studied Basia for a full thirty seconds.

She sensed he didn't believe her.

"That will make things slightly more difficult. And what about you, Alex?" Mr. Templeton asked. "There is a very real possibility of a countersuit against you for the method with which you gained this information."

"I don't care. If it helps Basia, if it stops Dr. Godfrey from hurting anyone else, whatever the price is will be worth it."

"You're a very strong young man. And you did your research well coming to me, if I do say so myself. But in your research you must have discovered that my rates aren't cheap. While this is a very noble cause, I'm afraid I can't offer any discount."

"We didn't expect you would. We're prepared to pay whatever it takes."

Mr. Templeton raised an eyebrow at that, obviously not believing Alex had such means available to him. "Is that so?"

"Yes, I've been working since I was fourteen and have saved most of it. I've never seen the need to live extravagantly, and Basia has been saving as well. We're prepared to pay your rate."

Mr. Templeton didn't look convinced, but let it go. "Very well. Of course, if you do win, that won't be a problem, since attorney fees will be included in the settlement."

"Winning is the only option, Mr. Templeton," Basia said. "If we go forward with this and lose, I'd rather kill myself than wait around for Dr. Godfrey to find me and make me suffer for this."

He studied Basia for a full thirty seconds. "I can see you mean that. In that case, I will have to work extra hard. Not that I wouldn't anyway, but as I've said, Dr. Godfrey is nearly untouchable in the medical community, and I'm sure he has much more money at his disposal for a team of lawyers than you do, no matter how much you've saved up."

"So you'll take the case?" Alex asked.

"Yes, I suppose I will. It's been a while since I had a real challenge. I welcome the change. I will have to take this to the police. These allegations must be reported to the authorities before I can do anything." They went over some paperwork, signed a contract that Basia barely understood, then shook hands and set another meeting for the following week.

"I didn't really want to move out on my own anyway," Basia said as they left the office.

"Basia, I don't want to sound too forward, or pressure you into anything that will make you uncomfortable, but if you want, you could move in with me. You don't need to be surrounded by so many people who scare you in what is supposed to be your home. You're going to be under enough stress. The least you deserve is a safe place to go home to at night."

"I won't be able to pay you. Mr. Templeton's retainer is going to wipe out everything I've saved."

"I don't care. I meant what I told him about money. It's not important to me. I just want you safe."

"Thanks, Alex. For once, I'm not going to argue with you. It would be really nice to have some privacy, and to not have to sleep with a knife under my pillow."

The next week, they met with Mr. Templeton again.

"Alex, you've done your homework quite well. I've been digging into Dr. Godfrey's past to see if I could turn up anything you might have missed, but it seems you have been very thorough. My research has allowed me to verify much of what you have given me from his work during the 70s. I agree, it was heinous. If he had truly stopped, he might have been forgiven. Things were much different back then, much less enlightened. But if the information on his recent experiments you have given me is true-"

"It is true!" Basia exclaimed.

"I don't meant to imply that it isn't, only that I can't verify it myself. As I was saying, with that information, I completely agree he must be brought to justice. So the first step will be presenting him with the lawsuit. I've drafted a document for you to review. Take it home with you and let me know what you think next week."

"That's it?"

"Basia, these things take time," Mr. Templeton said.

"So...once he's served, can I get a restraining order? For him and Dr. Schultz?"

"Yes, we can certainly file for one, and I don't think it would be too hard to convince a judge to grant it."

Basia relaxed.

"But you understand that doesn't always stop people from approaching those who have the restraining order?"

"Yes, I do, but it's better than nothing."

Alex chimed in, "I don't think Dr. Godfrey will do anything, at least not until this is all over. If he did, that would mar his reputation and tilt things in our favor a bit."

"Quite true," Mr. Templeton agreed. "Review the document, and we'll meet the same time next week." He shook both their hands before they left.

"I guess once this all gets rolling, I can finally tell my therapist and Dr. Tom the truth about everything. I'll certainly need it, I'm sure," Basia said. "She'll probably be upset with me for lying. I mean, how can she help me if she doesn't know the true problem?"

"I'm sure she'll understand. You weren't in a very good position."

"I hope you're right."

"The last thing she's going to do is lecture you, I'm sure. That probably wouldn't be very productive. Come on, let's go home."

Basia smiled as Alex put his arm around her shoulders. She'd moved her few belongings to his apartment the day after their initial meeting with Mr. Templeton. "Home. I like the sound of that."

CHAPTER 15

AFTER THE LAWSUIT WAS PRESENTED to Dr. Godfrey, Basia kept expecting the worst. Or at the very least she expected an angry phone call or letter or something - anything - from him. Maybe even from Dr. Schultz. But there was nothing. Not a whisper from either of them. He was even smarter than she'd expected. She supposed he knew she could record a phone conversation or save a letter as evidence during a trial.

Her nightmares, however, were growing worse. Every time she fell asleep, she relived scenes from her past with Dr. Godfrey. When it wasn't that, it was scenes as vivid as a movie of horrible experiments she was part of. She wondered if that's what had been done to her during her year in the abandoned asylum; the year of which she had no memory.

Because she couldn't sleep, Basia took on extra shifts at her job. Sometimes working double shifts, sometimes working ten days in a row. Sometimes both. She hoped it would make her so tired that she'd have dreamless sleep, but it didn't work. It only made her dreams worse.

One night in the middle of March, Basia arrived home from work while Alex was out. She was so exhausted, however, she couldn't wait for him to get home before she fell asleep.

She lay in a hospital bed, in a sterile white hospital room. Trying to get up, she discovered she was strapped down to the bed. Or was it an operating table? It was hard to tell in her fuzzy dream state. Whatever it was, she knew it wasn't good.

As she struggled against her bonds, Dr. Schultz came in and stuck a needle in her arm. "Morphine. This will help you to relax," he said.

Why was Dr. Schultz in her dream? Based on the situation, she couldn't imagine he was there to help her. "What are you going to do to me?"

"Oh, nothing for you to worry about. Just relax. You won't feel a thing. Well, you might, but that's not the point."

She looked down the length of her body and realized she was naked, which made her panic even more. Dr. Godfrey must be somewhere nearby, ready to use her as he had dozens of times already.

"Getting addicted already? Trying to make me give you more? Well, it's not going to work. My experiment has very little room for change. We must start at this level then work our way up."

"What experiment?" Basia wanted to scream for help, but somehow knew no one would hear her, or if they did, no one would come.

"I'm testing the effect of morphine on pain tolerance."

That didn't sound good. It looked even worse when he wheeled over a table with needles, scalpels, and what she assumed was surgical thread.

"I'll start with the needle again."

"Again?"

"Yes, don't you remember our session last week?"

Basia said nothing.

"Interesting. Perhaps your brain is protecting you from the memory of the pain. You did suffer greatly. The morphine should ease your suffering a bit today."

Dr. Schultz stuck Basia with a needle, just a tiny prick, then progressing deeper and deeper. She tried not to cry out, but small sounds of pain escaped her throat.

"Good, that is better than last week." The doctor tapped notes into his laptop.

Basia whimpered as he chose a scalpel from the tray, and she tried to struggle out of her bonds.

"Now now, the more you struggle, the worse this will be. Just relax," he said. First, he lightly dragged the scalpel across the top of her thigh, more of a tickling sensation than anything, leaving nothing but an irritated red line behind. Then he pushed harder, drawing blood and forcing Basia to cry out in pain. When she thought she couldn't take any more, he stopped. Maybe it was all over.

But she wasn't to be that lucky. Dr. Schultz moved to the other side of the operating table and pressed the knife deep into Basia's other thigh. When she screamed, he maintained the pressure and dragged the knife all the way down her thigh, creating a deep, six-inch incision that gushed warm blood all over the table. Basia screamed and screamed.

"That's nearly the same reaction you had last week. It seems this small dosage of morphine is good for small amounts of pain but does nothing against deeper pain. Well then, let's get you patched up." He cleansed the first wound and closed it with butterfly bandages, then wrapped it in gauze. The other leg still gushed blood, and Basia feared she would lose too much and pass out. The world was already blurry, and she couldn't focus.

Her focus was brought back front and center when the doctor stuck the first needle through her thigh and started stitching up the wound. She'd had stitches before, but always with local anesthesia. The feel of the needle tearing through her skin, then the awful sensation of the thread being dragged through the hole created by the needle made her cry and squirm and beg for the doctor to stop.

"But if I stop, you will surely bleed to death."

"Please, give me something for the pain."

"That's not part of the experiment. I want to record your reactions, untainted by anesthesia."

"Why are you doing this?" she asked when he finished and wrapped the other leg with gauze. "Don't you already know how morphine affects patients?"

"Of course, I've read about it, but I like to see things for myself. It means so much more with firsthand experience."

"You're sick."

Dr. Schultz ignored the comment and proceeded to Basia's arm. He tightened a strap just above her elbow then inserted a needle into *her vein. He attached a pint of blood.*

"Now what? Giving me some awful disease?"

"No. You've lost a lot of blood, and I want you strong and healthy for the next experiment," he said, then left the room while Basia remained strapped to the bed, in pain, and confused.

Basia woke screaming and sat straight up in bed. Alex rushed into the bedroom.

"What's wrong? Are you okay?"

She sat in bed rocking back and forth and crying, knees hugged to her chest. Suddenly, she realized her legs hurt. When she stretched out her legs she saw a bloody gash down the top of each thigh.

"Oh my god, what did you do to yourself?"

"No, no, it can't be real, it was just a dream, it's not real, make it stop," Basia babbled.

"What do you mean?" Alex tried to hold her still.

"The dream. He cut me. Just like this in the dream. But how is it real? Dreams can't be real." The sheets were covered in blood.

"Maybe you scratched yourself," Alex said.

Basia held out her hands to show how short her nails were and shook her head.

"I'm sure there's some sort of explanation. Come on, let's get you cleaned up and change the sheets."

While Alex tried to bandage her wounds, she realized they were exactly as they had been in her dream. He had to take her to the hospital to get stitches in her right thigh because the bleeding would not stop, no matter what he tried. The nurse at reception didn't believe her story about just waking up with the wound and eyed Alex suspiciously, but admitted her nonetheless. What else could she do - leave Basia to bleed to death?

Hours later, they finally left the hospital. Basia was on some strong pain medication and couldn't walk straight, but was still afraid to go back to sleep. Alex left her sitting on the couch while he changed the sheets.

"Basia, do you need to tell me something?" he asked when he was done.

Basia giggled, loopy from the pain medication. "You're cute."

"I'm serious. Are you trying to kill yourself?"

Maybe you should, the voice said to her. *Do it yourself before anyone else can kill you.*

She snorted with laughter. "No, Dr. Godfrey can do that all on his own. I don't need to help him," she slurred.

"I found this on the floor next to the bed." Alex held up a bloody scalpel.

"That's not mine, I didn't do it, I swear it isn't mine." Basia sat up straight on the couch, eyes wide.

Are you sure? You are crazy, after all.

"Then where did it come from?"

"The doctor in the dream. He cut me, he stuck needles in me then cut me with a scalpel. I was tied down, I didn't do it, it isn't mine."

"I can't help you if you don't tell me the truth Basia."

"I'm telling the truth," she said, tears falling down her cheeks. "I don't want to die, Alex, I swear, it wasn't me. It was the dream."

"You're not making any sense. Dreams aren't real. This scalpel had to have come from somewhere." He sighed. "Okay, let's get you to bed, and I'm going to stay with you and make sure nothing happens to you. We can talk about this tomorrow after the pain meds have worn off."

"It wasn't me," Basia said again.

"Just get some sleep, don't worry about it now." Alex helped her stand up from the couch and led her into the bedroom.

When she saw the bed, she started shaking and crying. "No, don't make me lie down there, he'll come for me again. He'll tie me down and hurt me."

"It's just our bed, Basia, nothing bad is going to happen to you. I told you I'll watch over your tonight."

"No, no, can't sleep there, can't sleep in the bed." She fought Alex as he tried to pull her to her feet.

"All right, all right, you can sleep on the couch. Just calm down, I don't want you to hurt yourself anymore."

"I didn't do it!" she screamed.

Alex stared at her for a moment, unsure how to respond. "Okay, you didn't do it. Please, Basia, just lie down and try to sleep. I don't know what else I can do for you right now."

She finally did as he asked and fell to sleep almost immediately.

CHAPTER 1°6°

THE NEXT DAY, BASIA CRIED out when she tried to pull her jeans on over her thighs. The wounds were too fresh, too sore, to have constrictive denim over them. She settled for wearing sweatpants to her therapy appointment. Work was going to be painful though. She had to wear the tan khakis. Maybe she could buy a pair a size or two too large and they wouldn't be as painful on her legs. Never mind that they'd fall down.

"I've heard of cases like yours," her therapist, Helen Federhofer, said after Basia finished her story. She'd also told Helen the full truth about her past with Dr. Godfrey and what had happened before she was committed.

"So you don't think I'm lying?" Basia nearly held her breath waiting to be believed.

"Not at all. I do think perhaps you don't remember bringing a scalpel home though." She stared Basia in the eye, as if expecting to find the truth there.

She thinks you're lying. Maybe you are. Maybe you're just useless at suicide.

"So what do I do? How can I make sure this doesn't happen again? I can barely even stand to wear pants the cuts are so bad."

"There's one thing we can try if you agree to it."

"What is it? I'll try anything, I'm so scared."

"We can try hypnosis to see if we can reach any memories you've hidden from yourself about the scalpel or what else may have happened." She looked at Basia, waiting for an answer.

The voice in her head just laughed at the absurdity of that suggestion.

"Do you know how to do that?" Basia asked.

"No, but I have a colleague whom I've worked with for years. He's very good, and I think you'll like him."

"When can we do this?"

"Are you sure you don't want to think it over?" Helen asked.

"No, I definitely want to do it. I want to know what the hell is happening to me. I need to know," she hoped the tears she felt pricking the corners of her eyes wouldn't fall.

"Okay, I'll call him and set up an appointment."

"Now?"

"I'll try. If he's with a patient, he won't answer, but I'll try." Helen picked up the phone. "Gregory, it's Helen. I need to schedule an appointment with you for a patient of mine." She paused. "Basia, is Friday at three okay?"

Basia nodded.

"That will be great, thanks, Gregory. I'll see you then." Helen hung up and pulled a business card from her desk drawer. "Here's his card with the address of his office. I'll meet you there on Friday. Do you have someone who could come with you? Sometimes, recipients of hypnosis are a little disoriented after a session, especially if the memories accessed are hard ones."

"Yes, I'm sure Alex will come with me."

"That's your boyfriend, right?"

The voice laughed harder. *Boyfriend. Sure, you can't even stand to have sex with him. I'm sure he'd just love that designation.*

"Well, I don't know about that. I'm not so great with physical affection, and the one time we tried to have sex, I completely freaked out."

"Relationships aren't always based on sex, Basia. In fact,

the best ones aren't. Sure, it's usually part of a romance, but not always. From what you've told me about him, I don't think he'd object to the 'boyfriend' label."

"I'd rather not deal with that right now. I'm overwhelmed as it is."

"I understand, Basia. We can work through your discomfort with intimacy later, when everything else has passed."

Basia didn't respond, not knowing what to say.

CHAPTER 17

BY FRIDAY, BASIA WAS EXHAUSTED. She'd been terrified to sleep and had only managed a few hours since Monday. She would only sleep when Alex was around to watch her and make sure she didn't hurt herself again. With Basia working nights though, that didn't happen often. So she just didn't sleep.

"Basia, we're here," Alex said when they reached Gregory Burrell's office, waking her up.

She groaned. "Sorry, I didn't mean to fall asleep."

"That's okay, you needed it. Do you feel up to this?" He turned in the driver's seat to look at her.

"Yes, I want to know what's going on."

Helen sat on a chair in the waiting room and stood to greet Basia. "You must be Alex," she said, extending her hand.

"Nice to meet you," Alex said.

"You can follow me into Gregory office. He's getting set up."

"Set up? What needs to be done?" Basia asked.

"Not much, don't worry, he's just making sure he has his recorder ready and note pad nearby."

"Recorder?" Basia repeated as they walked into the office.

The man in the office answered. "Yes, if you don't object, I'll record our session. I've found it very helpful in catching things that may have been missed in real time. Sometimes, the patient talks so fast I can't catch what she's saying, so I can replay it as many times as I need to in order to get everything transcribed and understand everything that has happened. By the way, I'm Gregory," he said, and Basia shook his hand.

"Nice to meet you," she said, voice shaking.

"We can just sit and chat for a few minutes if you like, see if you're comfortable and ready to do this. If you change your mind, that's okay; please don't hesitate to tell me."

Basia nodded.

"Helen has told me a little about your case, per the agreement you signed with her allowing her to do so. I'm sure she explained the knowledge is necessary for me to ask the right questions in order to find out what's going on."

"How does this all work?" Alex asked.

"Basia will lie down on the couch," he said, pointing to what looked to be a very comfortable overstuffed couch. "As I'm sure you've seen in movies, I'll count backward from ten with the lights dim so Basia can relax and get into a peaceful state of mind. Once she is under, I'll begin asking simple questions. Then I'll move onto questions more closely related to her case, then finally onto the most important questions to try to figure out what's going on."

"Helen, did you tell him everything, or just about what happened the other night?" Basia asked.

"Just about the other night. We'll see how this session goes, if you still want to do this, and how you feel afterwards before talking about going any more in depth."

"Okay, I'm ready," Basia said.

"Are you sure? Would you like anything to drink to help you relax before we start?" Gregory asked.

"No, I'm ready, I just want to get this over with. I mean, find out what happened."

"Okay, make yourself comfortable on the couch and I'll dim the lights. I'm going to turn on this noise machine that will help to drown out any background noise from outside the building. I've turned the ringer on the phone off so there should be nothing to jar you out of your state of relaxation once you enter it."

Basia got comfortable and felt as if she would immediately fall asleep. She willed herself not to, and waited for Gregory to start counting backward. As he did she was surprised to find herself feeling peaceful for the first time since...well, probably since before her dad had died. She felt a small smile on her face before everything faded.

As soon as the session started, she was woken up and brought back to complete consciousness. She no longer felt peaceful though. She felt as if a terrible omnipotent being were watching her every move and was somehow inside her head. She sat straight upright, drenched in sweat, heart racing, breathing shallow.

Alex was next to her in an instant, put his arm around her shoulders and pulled her close to him.

"What happened? Why do I feel so out of sorts? Did you already hypnotize me?"

"Yes, Basia, you were under for forty-five minutes."

"But I feel like I just laid down. I don't remember anything."

"That's common, don't worry."

"Is it common to wake up feeling so terrified and anxious?"

"Well, the memories we pulled from your mind were particularly violent, so yes, that isn't surprising."

"So what happened to me? Tell me," she demanded.

Gregory looked at Helen, who nodded for him to proceed.

"Well, it seems that somehow, some sort of psychic suggestion has been planted in your brain. I don't know how it is possible, but someone has tampered with your brain in such a way that they have implanted ideas for you to act upon at a given time, or upon a given trigger."

"But how is that possible?"

"I don't understand it myself, Basia, though I will research it and see what I can find out for you. I've never seen anything like it before," Gregory said.

"So someone fucked with my brain and made me cut

myself? Is that what you're telling me?" Tears rolled down Basia's cheeks.

"Yes, I'm afraid so," Gregory replied.

Well, look at that; you weren't lying after all. You're still useless at committing suicide though.

"Did you find out what else is in there? What else I'm going to do to myself or other people?"

"No, I did not. I haven't worked with anything like this before, so I'm going to have to try to figure out how to access that information. But I'll have to have your consent to do so, since it will be a brand-new venture for me, something I've never tried before. Something I don't know if anyone has tried before."

"I'll try anything, I just want this all to stop. Did you find who did this?" Basia's knee bounced up and down.

"I wasn't able to access that information. You didn't know who the person was. I can only get information you actually know from hypnosis."

"If we had pictures, would I be able to point the person out if I saw him?"

"I believe so, yes, though you would likely have to be under hypnosis again to do so. However, I don't even know where to begin in gathering a group of pictures for you to choose from."

"It had to have been Dr. Godfrey and Dr. Schultz. At the very least, they had to be involved somehow. Can we get pictures of all their known associates, no matter how loosely related, and can I try to choose from those?"

"Yes, we can try that."

"Well let's do it then. When can we meet again?" Basia asked.

"You should take at least a few days to recover."

"I don't want to wait, I want to know!"

"Basia, I'm sorry, I can't allow you to push yourself on this," Helen said. "It's too dangerous. You've been making wonderful progress, and I don't want you to be set back with all this. Please, take a few days. Maybe we can meet again next Wednesday?" she made it a question to Gregory, who checked his appointment book and nodded. "What time will work for you?" she asked Basia.

"It doesn't matter, you know I work nights, so any time during the day is fine."

"Okay, we'll meet next Wednesday at ten," Gregory said, writing it into his appointment book.

"Helen, would you go with me to my next appointment with Dr. Tom? I haven't told him the truth about any of this, and I think it will help if you're there to tell him about the hypnosis. I'm sure he'll be upset."

"Yes, I think in this case that would be helpful," Helen said.

"Thank you for helping me," Basia said before leaving. She was still shaky, and Alex helped her out to the car with an arm around her shoulder.

CHAPTER 18

THAT NIGHT, BASIA TRIED TO fight sleep again but was too exhausted to do so. She sat on the couch watching a scary movie, but that didn't work. She tried standing while watching the movie, also with no luck. Finally, she gave up and sat back on the couch and let sleep take her.

"You have come back to me," Dr. Schultz said.

"Why are you doing this to me?"

"I told you. Research. I want to see things for myself. But you are turning out to be far too clever for your own good, so I'm going to have to skip the middle of the experiment and go right to the end."

"What's that? Cutting me without any morphine at all?" Basia said, glad she sounded braver than she felt.

"Oh, no, I know what would happen with that. I was hoping to gauge your tolerance to pain before moving on to the final step, but I will just have to hope you can withstand the pain."

"And what if I can't?"

"Well, I guess that will be an interesting twist to the experiment. I don't know. I almost hope I find out. Though you have been far too fun, I hope that your escape won't be permanent."

"What do you mean escape?"

"You're trying to get away from me and my colleagues. You and *your friend are smart enough that you very well may be successful. But I hope to be able to track you down again sometime, when you least expect it. When no one expects it. Then we can continue where we left off."*

"Over my dead body."

"Oh, I hope not. Though I'm sure Dr. Godfrey knows some people who would be happy for that."

Basia thought she would throw up. "So what are you going to do to me?"

"I'm not going to tell you. That would ruin the surprise."

"I don't like surprises."

"Too bad for you." He came at her with a needle in hand and stuck her thigh before she could react.

Basia immediately felt groggy, and couldn't fight when he led her to the operating table and strapped her down again. She didn't know how much time passed before whatever he'd given her wore off and she felt fully alert again, though she had never fallen asleep completely. She wondered what would happen if she fell asleep in her dream. Would she wake up in real life?

With that thought, she realized this was a dream, and she could get out of it if she tried. Maybe all she had to do was fall asleep. She closed her eyes and tried to slow her breathing, trying to make her body listen to her will.

"Oh, that won't work. That's part of what I injected you with, something to prevent you from falling asleep. You're clever, but not that clever," Dr. Schultz said while he hooked another blood transfusion IV up to Basia's left arm.

"What are you doing?"

"Oh fine, I'll tell you if for no other reason than to make you stop asking. I'm going to slit your wrist. I want to know if the blood transfusion system we have works faster than you will bleed to death."

Basia remembered their last meeting and how it transferred to real life. Though she had a feeling there wouldn't be a transfusion hooked to her in real life, so if he slit her wrist she'd surely die. "No, please, you can't. I'll die if you do, you know that. You said yourself you wanted to find me in the future. If you do this now, you won't be able to because I'll die. I know somehow you're making me do these things to myself while I sleep, but there's no way you could have set up having an IV into my arm in real life so I won't die."

Dr. Schultz didn't react and continued his work. When he was finished, he chose a scalpel from the table and leaned over her.

"Please, don't!" Basia screamed. She continued screaming and screaming, hoping maybe her corporeal body would scream as well and wake Alex or the neighbors or something. Anything. But no one came to help her, and Dr. Schultz carefully, oh so carefully, sliced into the vein running the length of her arm while Basia continued to scream until her throat was raw.

When Basia woke, the world was fuzzy, and people surrounded her. "What..." she couldn't talk, her throat hurt.

"Don't talk, you're going to be okay," someone said, and the world bounced beneath her.

"Where am I?" Her voice came out as a whisper.

"We're wheeling you out of your apartment into an ambulance. We're going to take you to the emergency room and get you all fixed up. Try to relax." She realized it was a paramedic.

Basia looked down and saw her right arm covered in bloody bandages. "I didn't do this, please believe me, I was attacked."

So close. Too bad you chickened out at the end and started screaming for help.

Basia was starting to think maybe she really should kill herself. She wished the voice in her head would go away.

"Don't worry about that right now, all you need to worry about is trying to relax and letting us take care of you."

"Where's Alex?" Basia asked.

"Is that your boyfriend?"

"Um..." She didn't know how to answer. "My roommate."

"I don't know, he wasn't at home. Do you want someone to call him when we reach the hospital?" the paramedic asked.

"Yes." Basia felt fuzzy.

"Okay, just relax then. We'll make sure he knows where you are."

When Basia woke again, she was at the hospital, in a room with beeping monitors, and an IV in her arm slowly putting blood back into her body. Alex was in a chair right next to her bed.

"Basia, I'm so glad you're okay, I was so worried. The police called me, and I just knew something horrible had happened to you. Well, it's not what I thought, but what happened?"

"It was another of those dreams. Please tell me you believe I didn't do this on purpose."

"I believe you. Especially after being at the hypnosis session with you today, I believe you. But Basia, we're not going to be able to let you be alone when you sleep anymore. You almost died."

"Alex, I don't know who it is, but they know how this works. In my dream, I realized I was in a dream, and I tried to make myself wake up, but the doctor had given me something that would prevent the dream me from falling to sleep. Since I couldn't fall asleep in the dream, I couldn't wake up in real life to make it stop."

"Did Dr. Schultz cut you in the dream?"

Basia nodded. "He had me hooked up to an IV and said he wanted to see which was faster, if the IV would pump blood into me faster than I would bleed out, or if I'd die first. But Alex, there was no IV in the bedroom, I would have died no matter what. I don't understand. He said he wanted to find me again later in life to continue his experiments on me."

"Whoa, slow down. Relax. Maybe you should rest and tell me all this later."

"No, I have to tell you now, in case something else happens to me. You have to know everything that happened." Basia told him all about her dream and what the doctor had said. "They know who you are." Basia clutched Alex's arm.

"What do you mean?"

"Even in the dream, they know who you are and that you're helping me."

"It's okay, Basia, we knew they know I'm involved, that's nothing new."

"But if this crap was implanted in my brain when I was supposedly missing, that was before I met you. How would they have known about you then?"

The color drained from Alex's face, but he tried to keep his expression neutral. "I don't know, Basia. I really don't understand any of this. But we're going to figure it out. I promise you, I'll help you figure this all out."

"I'm scared what will happen to you though."

Make him leave. Don't make him suffer any more than he already has because of you.

"We've already talked about that, so stop worrying about me. I want to help you. I want to make sure you're going to be safe. Basia, I love you." Alex stopped. "I'm sorry, I shouldn't have said that, it's too much for you to hear right now."

"No, I just..." Basia felt a tear slip out of her eye and down her cheek.

Alex wiped it away. "Please don't cry. Forget I said anything. Just get some rest." He stood.

"Don't go. Please, don't leave me alone, I'm so scared." More tears fell.

He sat back down, hands in his lap.

"Hold my hand, please."

Alex did as Basia asked.

"Will you say it again? I want to know that you mean it, that I wasn't just imagining things."

Alex remained silent.

"If you didn't mean it, if it slipped out, please tell me, please don't leave me wondering about that. I can't take that right now, Alex."

"I love you, Basia. It did just slip out; I didn't mean to say it now, but it's true. I do love you."

Tears flowed from Basia's eyes. "I don't know if I can say it back. I think I love you, but I haven't known love in such a long time, I don't know what it feels like anymore."

"You don't have to say anything you don't want to. Just believe that I mean it and I'm not going anywhere."

"I love you too, Alex," Basia said, though she really wasn't sure what it truly meant. She wanted to love him, and maybe that was enough for now. "You'll stay with me if I fall asleep?"

"I promise. And if I have to leave for any reason, I'll be sure a nurse stays with you until I get back. I'm going to go home tomorrow and get my laptop and a change of clothes, then I'm going to stay here with you as long as necessary. I can do my work from here. I'm not going to leave you alone again until this is all over.

Basia squeezed his hand and closed her eyes, feeling safe.

CHAPTER 19

THE NEXT DAY, DR. TOM and Helen came to talk to Basia while Alex went to get his stuff from the apartment. Helen explained that she'd told Dr. Tom the truth about everything since Basia hadn't had another appointment with him since the hypnosis.

"Are you sure you didn't do it on purpose?" he asked.

Basia was tired of trying to explain what had happened. "Helen was there for the hypnosis session. You know what happened to me. Of course I didn't do it on purpose. If I had, would I have been screaming so loudly? I wanted someone to find me and save me. I was asleep, and I couldn't do anything to stop it."

"Calm down, Basia, I just have to ask. I have to make sure I know exactly what is going on, though I can't say I understand any of it."

"Has Gregory figured anything out yet?" Basia asked.

"It's only been two days. He hasn't had as much time as he'd like to research your situation," Helen said.

"Two days." It felt like longer. "It seems like this has been going on forever."

In a way, it has. And it will never stop.

"I know. We're going to get you through this. We'll do everything we can to figure out what's happening to you and to fix it. I promise," Dr. Tom said.

"I'm sorry if I seem impatient, but this is so scary. I know your business is understanding people, but you really can't understand exactly how terrifying this is."

"You're right, Basia, I can't, but I can try to imagine. I understand this is hard on you."

"I appreciate everything you're doing, and your believing me. Is there anything we can do to get Gregory more time to research this?"

"He's not scheduling any more appointments for the next week. He can't cancel what he already has, but he's doing his best," Helen said.

"I think Alex is trying to research it as well," Basia said. "He's really good at finding things out. He found out everything we needed about Dr. Godfrey. So maybe he'll find something on this too. Heck, maybe there was something in Dr. Godfrey's notes that he hasn't found yet."

"We'll keep doing all that we can. I'm not going to quit on you, Basia," Dr. Tom said, and Helen nodded agreement.

Basia was reluctant to believe them. Alex hadn't quit on her yet, but aside from that, life hadn't been kind to her, so she didn't want to get her hopes up.

The next day, she was released from the hospital after Dr. Tom had assured the staff that she wasn't a danger to herself. She had feared he'd want her to be committed again after finding out the truth, and was surprised he was so cooperative. The psychiatrist at the hospital did want to check Basia into a mental institution, but upon seeing the terror in Basia's face at mention of that, Dr. Tom convinced the doctor to do no such thing. He explained a bit about Basia's situation, leaving it at vagaries, and told him he was convinced sending her back to the mental institution would be a step backward, not forward, for her.

The next few weeks were excruciating for everyone involved. Dr. Tom, Helen, and Gregory worked long hours researching what could have been done to Basia's brain. Mr. Templeton was working hard to gather everything he needed for the case. Alex had told him what was going on and that they needed to move as quickly as possible or Basia's life might be at stake. Mr. Templeton told him he usually didn't expedite cases without a large extra fee, but when Alex showed him pictures of the cuts on Basia's legs and arm and the transcript of the hypnotherapy session, he agreed to expedite free of charge. Basia was thankful to have found a lawyer with a conscience.

It had been a year since Basia had woken in the abandoned asylum. Alex asked if she wanted to do anything to celebrate her freedom, but she didn't want to think about the situation. She just wanted to sleep, and made sure Alex would watch over her while she did.

"You're getting smarter," Dr. Schultz said as soon as Basia woke in dream land.

"Why do you say that?"

"Making sure someone watches over you while you sleep. Very smart. I can't make you do anything to hurt yourself when someone is watching. I guess it's a good thing we got to Alex even before we got to you."

Basia's stomach dropped. "What did you do to him? And how did you know I'd meet him?"

"You'd be surprised how adept we are at orchestrating people's lives. Our mind-control experiments have proven to be even more accurate than we had hoped."

"You're sick! You all need to be stopped!"

"You might succeed at stopping some of us, but there are so many more involved in this. It's a very carefully laid out system, such that no one person knows everyone who is involved, just in case something like the dilemma you have presented us should ever occur. So you may find out some of our names, and we will be out of the picture if you succeed, but there are dozens more that you will never know of, and they will train more, and so on."

"Why would you do this?"

"Can you imagine how useful this would be for governments? The ability to control soldiers, making them perform acts their morality might otherwise prevent them from doing? And our spy network, my

goodness how it will thrive! We'll be able to plant spies in foreign governments who don't even know they are spies until we set off the codes in their brains. The United States will be so powerful! And we will be rich from selling this knowledge to other countries."

"So the government is behind all this?"

"I didn't say that. The government knows nothing of this, aside from a few key agents who are necessary to the experiments. The government will only get involved when we are ready to sell this to them, at a discount, of course, as incentive for them to not put us all in jail for illegal experimentation."

"You really think they'll agree to that?"

"You put too much faith in your government, Basia. But back to the matter at hand. It appears you are healing quite nicely from our last meeting. Very clever of you with the screaming to alert your neighbors."

"You knew I'd do that, didn't you? But what if help hadn't arrived in time?"

"That's a risk I had to take. You think this time you'll be safe. I can hear it in the tone of your voice. Your precious Alex is watching over you. He won't let anything bad happen to you. Why he spends so much time on a girl who won't even let him fuck her, I don't understand."

"He loves me for who I am."

"If you say so. But he won't be able to save you this time."

"He's watching me. He won't leave me alone, so you won't be able to make me hurt myself."

Dr. Schultz jabbed Basia with a needle. "You are so naive. Now you won't be able to wake yourself up." He looked up and into the distance, seeing but not seeing whatever was in front of him. "And now Alex will have a sudden uncontrollable urge to go out to get lunch for the two of you. He'll know he shouldn't leave you, but he is going to call the order into the Chinese restaurant just down the street, thinking a mere ten minutes isn't enough time for you to hurt yourself. How wrong he is."

"Leave him alone!"

"Too late, the command has already been sent to his brain. He's already dialing the phone."

"What are you going to do to me this time? Try to kill me again?"

"No, you've proven quite adept at avoiding that. I'll wait a while before trying that again, if circumstances allow."

"So what?"

"I'm going to put a few more commands into your brain, rewire a few more neurons, if you will."

"Why?"

"Because it's fun."

Basia whimpered at the tools on the tray. "You'll get him arrested. If he comes back and my skull is cut open, there's no way to explain that."

"You think everything I do in this world has to be mimicked in real life. You have so much to learn."

"Then why make him leave?"

"Just in case you do manage to somehow gain a bit of consciousness and start screaming. I don't want him to hear and wake you up in the middle of the procedure here in dreamland."

"What would happen if he did?"

"That's a very good question. Perhaps we'll explore that one of these days. I don't know. But for now, I much prefer to make you suffer."

"Haven't you people made me suffer enough?"

"It's never enough, Basia, when will you learn that? Life is nothing but suffering. Sure, there may be some good moments here and there, but overall it's suffering. Surely you won't disagree?"

Basia said nothing, not sure what answer would be best. She couldn't honestly disagree with him, but didn't want to give him the pleasure of hearing her say he was right. She'd never say that.

"You know I'm right, even if you don't want to say so."

"There are plenty of people in this world who are happy."

"You think so? Can you read their minds? They're just lying to themselves. They put on a brave exterior, but inside they're screaming, as miserable as the rest of us." The doctor picked up an electric razor and shaved Basia's hair off, then moved on to the procedure to cut into her head and brain.

"Why can't I feel anything?" she gave in and asked, surprised he didn't want her physically suffering the pain of the procedure.

"As I said, I don't want you screaming in real life, so I gave you local anesthesia. I'd much prefer to watch you suffer, but this will be *quicker if you don't. And I don't have much time."*

"It will only take Alex ten minutes to pick up the food."

"So much to learn," Dr. Schultz said, almost to himself, but didn't explain further.

Basia tried hard to scream, but every time she opened her mouth and filled her lungs with air, nothing came out, as if she'd lost her voice. She could speak just fine, but screaming was out of the question. Even though she felt no physical sensation, the sounds of the doctor cutting through her skull and poking around in her brain were unbearable enough. She cried silently, wishing he'd slip and cut something vital and kill her in the process. But he was too skilled for that.

After what felt like days, he finally finished the procedure and stitched her back up.

"Do you have something to do with the voice in my head?" Basia asked when he was done.

"Voice? No, I can honestly say that I don't. Interesting." The doctor turned to the table to make a few notes. "How long have you been hearing this voice?"

"Why should I tell you?"

"I need to know if it is a result of our experiments," he said.

"Why do you think I would help you? Why should I tell you anything?" Basia struggled against her bonds, and finally woke up.

"Hungry?" Alex asked when she sat up.

"You promised not to leave me alone."

"I know, but I made sure there was nothing around that you could harm yourself with, and I wasn't even gone ten minutes."

"But what if the doctor could have done something else to me?"

"Like what?" He scooped some rice and orange chicken onto a plate for Basia.

Basia tried to form words to explain what had happened while she slept, but she couldn't. "Like, I don't know, somehow...doing something..." she trailed off, some mental aversion to forming a complete sentence.

"You seem fine to me," Alex said. "Are you?"

Again, Basia could not say no, no matter how hard she

tried to, so she simply nodded once.

CHAPTER 20

"WE'RE JUST ABOUT READY TO go to court," Mr. Templeton said the next day when they met. "I'm going to file for a court date this afternoon."

"That's great news," Alex said. "Basia, are you going to be okay?"

Basia had been silent and distant through the whole meeting, still reeling from the night before. She'd already taken two Xanax that day to no avail. The thought of confronting her tormentors in court was enough to send her over the edge, and the panic attack she'd been trying so desperately to fight off finally won. She started shaking and couldn't breathe.

You'll see him in court, and then you'll have proof of how truly helpless you are against him.

"Basia, try to take slow, deep breaths," Alex coached. That never worked, though it usually prevented her from hyperventilating and passing out.

This time, it did nothing. She tried to take a deep breath but felt like a fish out of water, gasping for oxygen. The world went fuzzy.

The next thing Basia knew, she was on a couch in the waiting room with a paramedic standing over her. She blinked a few times to clear her vision and took a breath, relieved that she was able to breathe again.

"How do you feel?" the paramedic asked.

"Tired. Head hurts."

She looked around while he took her blood pressure and temperature. Alex was pacing across the room while Mr. Templeton sat in a chair waiting patiently for whatever was going to happen. She supposed he was used to all sorts of drama from the courtroom, leaving him capable of dealing with stressful situations with ease. She wondered if anyone had ever passed out in his office before, and if he worried about a lawsuit. She almost laughed at that last thought.

"Everything looks okay. Do you want to go to the hospital?" the paramedic asked.

"No! I'm fine, no hospitals, please."

"I'll need you to sign this waiver stating you refuse further attention," he said as he handed her a piece of paper.

She signed it happily, never wanting to see the inside of a hospital again.

"I know you've both spent a great deal of time and money on this case, but are you absolutely sure you are up to continuing?" Mr. Templeton asked once the paramedics had left.

"Basia, he's right, that's the worst episode you've had since I've known you. Maybe you should reconsider this if it's too stressful for you," Alex said.

"No way. Not going forward would be even worse, fearing Dr. Godfrey for the rest of my life. I'll be fine, we have to do this. We can't stop now."

"If you're absolutely certain..." Mr. Templeton said.

"Are you afraid I'm going to sue you because I passed out in your office? Is that what this is about?"

"Of course not. I've just never seen anyone have such a strong reaction to anything."

"It's not just that. It's just been a very stressful couple of months, and I haven't been sleeping well." That much was the truth. "And there's something else."

Mr. Templeton crossed his arms. "Basia, if you've left

anything out in all this time, it could greatly affect the case."

"No, it just happened. Last night."

Alex jerked his head toward her, eyes wide.

"I had another dream last night." She told them what Dr. Schultz said about the mind control experiments and plans to sell the capability to governments around the world.

"Why didn't you tell me last night?" Alex asked.

"I couldn't. Something was preventing me from saying anything. But now, I don't know if my panic attack affected something, I have no idea, but I was suddenly able to tell you about it."

"I don't know if I'll be able to use this, Basia. I hope you understand that dreams are not proof of anything."

"I do, I just thought you both should know about it, just in case it can help somehow."

"All right then, I'll request a court date this afternoon as planned. I'll be in touch when we need to meet again." Mr. Templeton stood and shook both their hands, seeming to be careful not to squeeze Basia's too hard.

She hated that he thought she was so weak, but what did his opinion matter? In a way, she was incredibly weak. Someone was manipulating her thoughts and actions, and she was powerless to fight it.

Basia didn't argue when Alex helped lead her out of the office and to the car, wanting nothing more than for everything to just end.

Basia discovered that the doctor had implanted the desire to self-harm, cutting herself almost to the point of needing stitches, but never quite going that far. Somehow, she was always able to bandage herself up before Alex noticed anything was wrong, and found herself unable to tell him what was going on.

"*How are you enjoying your newfound coping mechanism?*" Dr. Schultz *asked a few days after the meeting with Mr. Templeton.*

"*I hope something terrible happens to you,*" Basia replied. "*And what are you doing to Alex? Are you as deeply in his mind as you are mine?*"

"Yes, but he doesn't know it. We used a different procedure with him, not wanting him to be aware of our manipulations."

"Is that why he isn't questioning why I suddenly wear long sleeves all the time?"

"Of course. There's a tiny voice in the back of his mind questioning your well-being, but we don't allow him to act upon that concern. Now, what shall I make you endure next? As exciting as it is to watch you mutilate yourself, I think we're ready for something different."

"We?"

"You think I'm the only one able to see through your mind? I see clearest since I'm the one who was planted there, but my colleagues are able to able to access your thoughts in a less direct manner."

"What do you mean?"

"I'm essentially in your head, with access to each and every one of your thoughts - even the ones you aren't aware of. My colleagues are only able to get electrical impulses translated into English. So their access isn't as direct, but is still fascinating to them. I fill in the missing details when necessary."

"Basia, Basia, wake up, you're having a nightmare."

"No!" Dr. Schultz yelled. "Stay with me, I'm not finished with you yet."

"Wake up!"

Basia heard the frantic words faintly, as if she were underwater. Then she became aware that someone was shaking her.

"Looks like you're losing your hold on me," she said before waking up.

Her eyelids fluttered as she fought to regain consciousness, then she blinked up at Alex several times. "Alex?" she asked, disoriented from being jarred from the nightmare.

"Yes, it's me. You were thrashing around in bed. Are you okay?"

Basia shook her head. "He did something to me."

"Who?"

"Doctor," she mumbled, surprised she was able to say anything.

"What did he do?"

"Can't say. Need to see Gregory." The aversion to saying

anything about the doctor's dreamland visits was coming back. "Hypnosis, maybe I'll be able to say then. Must see him now."

"Basia, you're not making any sense."

"Please, Alex!" she shouted in frustration. "Call Gregory, it's urgent." She was afraid if she waited too long the aversion would be back full strength and she wouldn't be able to say anything even under hypnosis.

"Okay, I'm calling him right now," Alex said while fishing his phone out of his pocket.

Thirty minutes later, they were at Gregory's office, and Basia was ready to be hypnotized again. "Ask me if there's anything I can't say when I'm awake," she told Gregory, surprised she could get that much out.

She woke to find Alex sitting on the floor next to the couch, holding her hand, tears streaming down his face. "Basia, I'm so sorry, I had no idea. Can you ever forgive me?"

"Of course, it wasn't your fault."

"But why would I have let you do that to yourself? I swore I wouldn't leave you alone while you were sleeping. How could I have not noticed that was happening?"

"Alex, you-" Basia stopped, unable to say anything else.

"I what?"

"The doctor-" Again, she couldn't finish the sentence. So she wasn't breaking free of his hold, at least not completely.

"What's wrong? Why can't you tell me?"

"He won't let me," she said, starting to cry.

"How do we get this sick bastard out of Basia's head?" Alex demanded from Gregory.

"I don't know, that's what I'm trying to figure out. Nothing like this has ever been accomplished before, so I have nothing but some sparse theoretical papers to go on."

"But you have to have some idea, something you can try," Alex said.

"I don't want to make any rash decisions that might do more harm than good."

"Look at her! Do you think you can do much more harm than she's already suffered? That sick bastard is controlling her, has manipulated her brain to make her do things she doesn't want to, wouldn't otherwise do. What can be worse than that?" Alex's hands were in fists at his sides, shaking.

"Alex, it's you too." Basia finally managed to say.

"What do you mean?" He stared at her, face blank with confusion. "Oh, god, do you mean he's in my head too?"

Basia couldn't respond, couldn't even nod.

"If I ever get my hands on that bastard, I'm going to kill him."

"Alex, calm down," Gregory said. "I'm sure you don't mean that, you're just angry right now."

"No, you're right. But how would you feel if someone had manipulated your brain?"

"I understand, but let's try to think through this logically. Do you know when he could have gotten to you? Have you ever been in the hospital for an extended period?"

"No, nothing more than a broken arm." Alex shook his head.

"Are you sure? There must have been some time when this doctor could have had access to you and time enough to do whatever it is that he does," Gregory prodded.

"I'm sure. I think I'd remember something like that."

"What about when you were a child?"

"No. Wait, I had tubes put in my ears when I was four, but that wasn't a long stay, just outpatient, and my parents were there the whole time, I think."

"It would have to be something longer than that. Did you have any health problems when you were a baby?"

"I don't think so."

"You don't sound certain," Gregory said.

"I'd have to ask my mom, I don't really remember." Alex shook his head. "I'll call my mom today. But what can you do to help Basia?"

"It would be best if we knew exactly what these doctors did to Basia. But I can try some hypnotic suggestions to help Basia become more resistant to the doctor's tampering."

"And if that doesn't work?"

"Well, then we'll have to try to convince Dr. Schultz to tell us exactly what they did," Gregory said.

"Gregory, when can you start? Can you do that today while Alex is tracking down the information we need for him?" Basia asked.

"Yes, I'll need to finish up a bit of research. I have almost everything in order that I'll need, but I just want to go through it all one last time. You understand I've never done anything like this before, and I don't know what the outcome will be?"

"I understand."

"I don't just mean that I'll be unsuccessful. I mean that I'm going to be putting some pretty strong suggestions into your thought process. It isn't as invasive as what the doctor did to you, and while I don't think there will be adverse affects, I can't guarantee that. Something like what I'm going to attempt has never been tried, or at least not documented."

"I understand, but I'm willing to do anything it takes to make this all stop."

"All right then, how about you get some lunch, then come back around one and we'll get started?

"Can I use your phone to call Helen? I'd like her to go with me, and be here if you don't mind."

"I don't mind at all. In fact, she should be here any minute. I called her as soon as I knew you were coming, but she was in St. Louis for a conference. She left when I told her what was going on."

"Thanks for everything you've been doing, Gregory."

CHAPTER 21

"I TALKED TO MY MOM," Alex said when the met back up. "When I was a baby, I had some kind of neurological condition, and they had to do surgery on me for it. She seemed reluctant to talk about it."

"It was probably hard on her, having to deal with something like that when you were so little."

"I guess, but I wonder if there's something more she isn't telling me. I'll have to try to find out. But I guess they could have gotten to me then, which means they've been planning all this for at least twenty-two years." Alex stared into Basia's eyes when he said this.

"I didn't think I could get any more scared than I already was."

He stroked her hair, longing for comfort as much as she.

Gregory cleared his throat. "If you're ready..."

"Yes, sorry. I'm definitely ready to get this over with and put it all behind me," Basia said.

As was always the case, Basia remembered nothing from the hypnotherapy session when she awoke. "So how did it go? What happened?"

"I think it went well, but we will only know in time if it

112

worked or not, and to what extent," Gregory said.

"What do you mean 'to what extent'?" Basia asked.

"Well, as I said, no one has ever done this before, so it is experimental. It could be that we have partially broken Dr. Schultz's hold on your mind, but not completely."

"What does that mean?"

"I'm sorry, but I just can't say, Basia. Maybe he can't control you anymore but can still communicate with you. Maybe he can only control you to a lesser extent. I wish I had a better answer, but we'll just have to wait and see how it all turns out."

"Should I even bother to ask how long we'll have to wait before we know anything?"

Gregory shook his head.

"Great. So something may have happened, or nothing, and who knows when I'll know." Basia sighed. "I'm sorry, I appreciate everything you've done, it's just terribly frustrating."

"I understand. It is also hard to say because the frequency of Dr. Schultz's visits to you is sporadic. So just because he does not contact you tonight when you sleep does not mean this worked. It may just mean he had no plans to contact you."

"I'm going to bet he did though. He must know what's going on, what we did, if he's as much in my head as he says he is. So if I don't hear from him tonight I'm going to take that as a good sign that we made some progress."

"Just don't get your hopes up too high too soon," Gregory said.

"I know. Hoping isn't something I'm good at anyway."

"So what now?" Alex asked.

"Now you go home and try to relax, and we see what happens," Gregory said.

"You know, one of these days I'm going to turn you into an optimist," Alex said to Basia on the way home.

"Ha. Good luck with that. Nothing has ever gone right in my life ever, so what should I be optimistic about anyway?"

"Nothing?" Alex's voice was soft and cautious, but with a

hint of sadness.

"Well, you're still around, so I guess not nothing. Though I'm still waiting for you to get sick of all this."

"Basia, if I haven't given up on you now, and as much as I've done to help you, why would I quit now?"

"I don't know. Please don't be upset with me, you've had a pretty good life. I haven't. Everyone leaves me, always. Even if you don't leave me by choice, I'm terrified Dr. Godfrey will find a way to tear you away from me, just like he's done with everyone else I loved."

"I know," Alex said with a sigh. "Look, let's just pick up some Chinese and go home and try to get some sleep."

"I'm still scared to sleep, Alex."

"I'll stay awake. It may not be the best defense, but it's better than nothing."

Alex reclined against the headboard, working on his laptop while Basia tried to sleep. She was terrified of what might be waiting for her when she did, and had to force herself to slow her breathing. When she finally drifted off, she found herself in the same room as she had previously been in with Dr. Schultz. This time, however, she wasn't tied down to the bed. She was standing, and wearing her own clothes rather than a hospital gown.

"*You grow stronger. Soon, I won't be able to communicate with you this way,*" Dr. Schultz said.

"*That's kind of the point,*" Basia said. "*I'd prefer if you don't communicate with me at all. In fact, I might prefer if you just disappeared.*"

"*I wouldn't recommend you say anything like that when you're awake. I'd hate for you to become the suspect in a missing person case.*"

"*Oh shut up, you'd love to see more tragedy befall me. So what are you going to do to me tonight? Try to make me kill myself again? Or maybe try to make me kill Alex? He's lying right next to me you know.*"

"*I think you know very well none of those are options any longer. Unfortunately, your hypnotherapy session with your precious Gregory worked, to an extent. Though I think you'll be dismayed to find out it is only a temporary solution."*

"Why would you tell me that? Don't you think I'll just keep going to him for as long as it takes to get you out of my head for good?"

"Ah, but nobody knows how his sessions will affect you. Maybe they'll get me out of your head, but what else will you lose in the process? Your intelligence, little that it is? Your memories?" He paused. "You humanity?"

"You know the answer, don't you?"

"Do you think you and Alex are the first people we've experimented on? Of course not. I know exactly how this will end."

"But I guess you're not going to tell me, are you?"

"That would take all the fun out of this. You've already taken some of the fun away."

"Well it's a risk I'm willing to take, if I get rid of you and Dr. Godfrey and all the rest."

"You're turning out to be quite brave. I have to say we didn't expect that from you."

"Why is Alex a part of this?" She hesitated to ask the next question. "Does he even really love me?"

"Unfortunately, we can control people's action, and to an extent suppress their emotions, but we cannot create emotions that do not already exist to a small extent. So yes, Alex does really love you. Which makes our experiments all the more interesting."

"But how did you know he and I would cross paths?"

"We didn't. We started experiments on him simply because he was easy to get to. His mother couldn't afford the surgery he needed as a child, and she was all too eager to avoid asking questions when we offered to cover the expense. When Dr. Godfrey met your mother, we decided it would be interesting to add you into the mix."

"But I was just a child."

"Yes. We didn't know how we would include you in the experiments, only that we wanted to. The details came later as you grew older."

"Was it an accident that he was near when you kidnapped me?" Dr. Schultz shook his head.

"So I guess it wasn't an accident that we met when we did either, was it?"

"Now you're starting to get it. We've done many experiments

with controlling individuals, and with groups of potential soldiers, but this is the first time we've caused two of our subjects to interact on a purely social level. It has been quite fascinating, and with more development could have many applications in politics."

"I'll find a way to stop you all."

"Best of luck to you. Many have threatened, but no one has yet succeeded."

Basia forced herself to wake up and found herself shaking in Alex's arms.

"What happened?" he asked.

Basia told him of the dream.

"So it worked, at least a little. That's great news! But everything else about the other experiments he said they've done is pretty scary."

"And what about what he said about what else I'll lose when I banish him from my head? My humanity is one of the things he mentioned. What if he meant that?" Basia said.

"Let's just take one step at a time. We'll tell Gregory about all that so he can be extra careful. I'm going to take care of you, Basia. If I have any say in the matter, I won't let anything bad happen to you."

"But what about you? You're going to have to go through this too. So just in case, I don't want you to do any hypnotherapy until I've been through it for a few months. If something is going to get screwed up in my brain in the process, I don't want the same thing to happen to you. Promise me that, Alex?"

"You don't have to be the guinea pig," he said.

"But I already am, don't you see? I've already been though it once, and will keep going through it. If something bad is going to come from it, there's no use both of us getting screwed up. I've already started, so let me stick with it."

"For how long?"

"I don't know. A few months? If nothing bad has happened to me, you can start working with Gregory too."

Alex sat straight up in bed. "Basia, that's just ridiculous. If they can make me leave when you're sleeping, I need them out of my head as badly as you do. Who knows what else they can make me do?"

"You don't have to be so mean about it," Basia said, staring into her lap.

"You don't have any right to tell me what to do. I want them out of my head, and I'm going to do this. It's the least I deserve after wasting so much time and money taking care of you."

"What are you saying, Alex? This isn't like you." Tears fell from Basia's eyes.

Alex took a few deep breaths. "Shit, Basia, I'm sorry. I didn't mean any of that. I don't know why I said that." He reached for her hand.

"Maybe it wasn't you talking."

"If that's true, it's even more important for Gregory to help me too."

"But I don't want you to get hurt in any way from this. Will you wait just a little while? Please?" Basia folded herself against him.

"I don't like it, but I guess you have a point. All right, I'll wait a little while."

The next day, Mr. Templeton called Alex to tell him the court date had been set. It wouldn't happen for another four months, at the beginning of August.

"So what do we do now?" Basia asked when he hung up.

"We wait. There's nothing we can do other than go on with our lives and wait. Mr. Templeton said he's surprised we got a date as soon as we did, that it usually takes a year or two for a date to be set. I bet it had something to do with Dr. Godfrey's influence."

"Well, at least we can thank him for something, I guess. Though without him this wouldn't be necessary in the first place."

"Basia, I've been thinking. I know a guy who's looking for a secretary. It would pay better than your cleaning job and be easier on you physically. If you're interested, I could let him know. He owes me a favor, so you'd be a shoo-in."

"Alex, I don't think that's a good idea. I've spent so much

time working on this bullshit in my head with Helen, I haven't had any time to work on my social anxiety. I'd be dealing with people all day there, right?"

Alex nodded.

"I don't think I can do that. Just thinking about it freaks me out big time. And anyway, I like the cleaning job. You know cleaning soothes me, so it's pretty much the perfect job for me right now."

"It was just a thought."

"I appreciate it, Alex, but I just can't handle that right now. Maybe after the trial when things have calmed down I can try something like that. I have been thinking though..."

"What?" Alex asked when she paused and didn't continue. "You can tell me."

"I've been thinking about going back to school. Maybe just some online courses or something."

"I think that's a great idea. Why would you hesitate to tell me?"

"Well, I know this case is costing a lot of money, and it doesn't seem fair for me to spend money on something for myself when you're probably draining your savings account dry to help me with this."

"Well that's the other thing Mr. Templeton just said. He said he isn't going to charge us anymore for his work on the case. He realizes we both got the short end of the stick here and doesn't want to ruin our lives by taking all our money. I know, an honest lawyer, can you believe it?"

"Wow. What's the catch?"

"There is none. He has something written up saying as much that we can sign so he can't go back on his word. So. What do you want to go to school for?" Alex smiled.

"I like the idea of being a teacher, but again...my anxiety. Kids can be the worst."

"I think you should go for it. You're going to get past all this, I just know it. You deserve something really great in your life for a change. Do what you want, I know you'll be able to handle it when the time comes. Besides, you can always change your major." He laughed.

"I guess you're right. Will you help me get started?"

"Of course I will. Let's sign you up right now. The next semester starts in a few weeks, so this is great timing."

"Alex, I really hate to say this because I know it's going to come back to bite me on the ass, but for the first time in my life, I think things may actually be starting to look up for me. And it's all because of you. Seriously. How can I ever thank you?"

"Well, you can start by letting me slit your wrists so I don't have to waste my time worrying about you anymore."

"What? Why would you say that?" Basia leaned away from him.

"Oh shit, Basia, I'm sorry. Shit. I really didn't mean that." Alex shook his head back and forth hard enough that Basia thought he'd give himself a concussion. Alex sat on the couch clutching his head. "Get out of my head, you bastard!" he yelled and threw his laptop across the room.

"Alex, it's all right, I didn't think, didn't realize...I know you wouldn't deliberately hurt me," Basia said, trying to calm him down.

But now they're working on him, so maybe he will hurt you. You see, it's dangerous to get close to anyone, no matter what.

"Don't you see? That's the point. I wouldn't deliberately hurt you. But that asshole is still in my head, trying to make me do things I don't want to do to you. It's not safe for me to be around you. They made you cut yourself while you were asleep. Why wouldn't they make me hurt you while I'm sleeping?"

"What are you saying?"

"I should find somewhere else to live until this is all over. It's not safe for you to be near me."

"Please don't say that, Alex, I don't have anyone else. You can't leave me!" Tears streamed down her face.

"I'm not leaving you for good, I'm just trying to keep you safe." Alex stood.

"Leaving me alone isn't going to keep me safe. What if Dr. Schultz comes back in my dreams, what if he gains control of me again? Who knows what I'll do to myself if he does. Please,

Alex, please don't leave me alone."

"Look at me, Basia, look what I just said to you. I don't have control over myself."

"We know what's going on now though, that has to mean something to you. Maybe you'll say things, but I'll know you don't mean it, and once you're aware of what's happening you can stop it."

"But what if I can't? What if he tries to make me really hurt you?" He paced in front of the couch.

"I'm willing to take that chance if it means you won't leave me alone."

"What if I'm not? Basia, if I did something to really hurt you, I wouldn't be able to live with myself. I'm not willing to risk that."

"So you're just going to leave me alone, just like that, to fend for myself against this sicko?"

"I don't know what else to do, Basia."

"This is a really fine way of turning me into an optimist. As soon as I say I think things are looking up, you decide you're going to leave. Thanks a lot, Alex, that's really helping me."

"Would you rather I stay so I can be part of Dr. Godfrey's sick plan and make it even harder to learn to cope with your depression and anxiety? Because if that's what you want, then fine. I'll cut you. Right now."

"Alex, would you listen to yourself? Just shut up and think about what you're saying. Do you really mean any of this?"

"Don't tell me to shut up. You're the one asking for me to stay and help you kill yourself."

Basia slapped him as hard as she could, leaving a red handprint on his cheek.

Alex stared at her. "This is what I'm talking about," he said. "I can't control myself. You'll be better off without me for a while."

Basia reached out for him, wanting to pull him to her, but he dodged her and went into the bedroom where he started packing a duffel bag.

"I'm sorry, Basia, but I really think this is for the best right now. I'll call Helen, maybe she'll know someone who can stay with you."

"I don't want a stranger watching me while I sleep. That's even worse than whatever Dr. Schultz might make me do. I know you mean well, Alex, but just stop talking. I'm going for a walk, and if you're really leaving, then I don't want to see you here when I get back."

CHAPTER 22

PEOPLE POINTEDLY AVOIDED BASIA AS she walked down the street, tears streaming down her face, but she didn't care. She'd been waiting for this to happen, so she wasn't sure why she was so surprised that it finally had. She shouldn't have allowed herself to believe that Alex just might stick around, that maybe something could go right for her for a change. That's why she never allowed herself to hope. If you didn't expect anything from people, they couldn't let you down. But now, she was nursing another broken heart.

Sure, he said it was only temporary, that he'd come back when this was all over with. But she'd made him promise not to try hypnotherapy for at least a few months. And what was she going to do alone in that time? She was truly scared of Dr. Schultz regaining control over her. If there was no one to watch over her while she slept, she could do anything to herself. Well, at least she wouldn't be able to hurt Alex since he wouldn't be around. And no way she was having a stranger stay with her.

Because strangers are almost as dangerous as people you know.

She walked for an hour and found herself downtown. She decided to stop and get a coffee, wanting to give Alex plenty of time to get out. If he was leaving, she didn't want to see him at all. They hadn't left things on the best of terms, but either he'd understand, or he didn't mean what he'd been saying the whole time. Either way, going back wouldn't do any good. It would only make her hurt more.

Maybe she'd be able to convince Gregory to do another session with her in the next day or so. Or maybe she should talk to Helen about all this before doing anything. Or maybe she should just give up. What was it worth anyway, all this fighting, all this suffering? What would she have in the end? Nothing, most likely. Nothing but more heartache and loneliness.

Maybe it was better that Alex was leaving now, before Basia had too much time to think things might actually work out. It was easier now than it would be a few months down the road. Sure, it hurt, but she'd get over it. That's what she had to keep telling herself. Just keep repeating that, and eventually she might even believe it. She'd been alone for so long, why not even longer? It wasn't so bad...no one to worry about, no one to call if you were going to be late.

Basia didn't really believe that though, and watched the tears fall from her chin into her coffee cup.

Alex was gone by the time Basia got back to the apartment hours later. He'd left a note on the kitchen counter saying that Helen would call Basia to work out a safe situation for her. Basia realized she'd left her phone behind, and had several missed calls from Helen. She was too tired to deal with it just then, and sat on the couch where she fell asleep.

"*Back already?*" *Dr. Schultz said.*

"*Not by choice.*"

"*Poor Basia, left alone again. Everyone leaves you...why did you expect otherwise?*"

"*I didn't.*"

"*You can't lie to me. Just because I can't control you anymore doesn't mean I don't still see all of your thoughts. I know you secretly hoped that Alex would never leave you, even believed it. I know you hoped you might even marry him someday.*"

"I did not!"

"Oh, but you did, even if you never admitted it to your conscious mind. It was there, obvious to those who knew where to look, and I knew exactly where to look. But you're alone again, and no one will be able to save you from me."

"You said yourself you can't control me anymore."

"But for how long? Don't you wonder? I know you're going to try to see Gregory tomorrow, but do you think he'll agree to another hypnotherapy session so soon?"

"He has to! He'll see how important it is."

"Is that so? He's very responsible and careful in his job, very meticulous. I think he will want to give it at least a few more days to see how you react to his treatment."

"You - you aren't in his mind too, are you?" Basia was horrified at the thought.

"Of course not, but some people are easy to read. I am very good at reading people, and I think he will wait."

"So are you saying you'll regain control before he does another session with me?" Basia asked.

Dr. Schultz only shrugged.

"Tell me, you bastard!"

"Sweet dreams, Basia," he said as he faded from her dream.

Basia didn't wake though. As much as she fought, she remained trapped in sleep, trapped with her nightmares. She dreamed of all the terrible things Dr. Schultz had already made her do. She dreamt she cut her legs again, dreamt she cut her wrist, and this time she couldn't scream, couldn't do anything but lie in bed and watch herself bleed. She kept bleeding until the bed was surrounded by a pool of blood, more blood than could come from one person, but still it poured from her wrist and thighs.

As Basia continued to scream and bleed and cry, the room continued to fill with blood until she was certain the bed would be carried away in the river of it. Somewhere in the back of her mind, she knew that it was a nightmare, and if she could just wake up it would all stop, but no matter how she tried she could not force herself to wake. She was to endure the terrible dream to its end, though she wasn't sure it would ever end.

She started to choke on the blood as it rose over the bed. It surrounded her and almost covered her. She struggled to sit up as it covered her face, but somehow Alex was now there, holding her down as she coughed and choked and gasped for breath until finally the world went dark.

She woke to find Alex leaning over her, his mouth on hers. She pushed him off as hard as she could and screamed at him to leave her alone.

"Basia, relax, I'm not going to hurt you."

"Get off me, you fucking asshole! Don't you dare touch me!"

Alex stood and backed to the opposite side of the room. "Okay, I can't touch you from here. Can you tell me what's wrong?"

"You're what's wrong, you sick fuck."

"Basia, you were having a nightmare. I realized I'd made a mistake in leaving you and came back, and you weren't breathing. I was giving you CPR, that's all. I promise."

Basia took a few moments to catch her breath and saw that Alex was fully clothed, though there was some blood on his clothes. "Who's blood is that?"

"Yours," he said.

She looked down at her arm and legs and saw that she had scratched bloody gouges into herself. At least it was just from her nails, and not a scalpel, and weren't deep enough to require medical attention. When she finally realized it had all been a nightmare, and that Alex had come back for her - to help her, not suffocate her - she reached out for him, wrapped herself around him, and cried. When she finally stopped crying enough to breathe normally, she told him all about the dreamland visit from Dr. Schultz, and the nightmare that followed.

CHAPTER 23

BASIA MET WITH HELEN AND Gregory the next day to discuss what her possible options might be. Was the nightmare a result of the hypnotherapy? And if so, would nightmares be a permanent or temporary side effect? Gregory thought it would be temporary as Basia subconsciously expelled her demons from her mind while she slept, and agreed to continue hypnotherapy with her. Helen wasn't so sure, but ultimately they left the decision up to Basia.

"And what about Alex?" she asked. Alex had dropped her off, sensing that she might want to have this meeting without him, and also needing some time to himself to process what had happened the previous night.

"What about him?"

"We agreed to wait a while before you did any sessions with him to make sure there wouldn't be any really bad side effects, but isn't there something you can do for him to make him not want to keep hurting me? After last night, he realized I really can't be alone until we're further along, and he agreed to stay, but it's going to be really uncomfortable if he can't partially control himself. He's scared of doing something to really hurt me."

And you know he will. They all do, in the end.

"Well, I can try traditional hypnotherapy and plant the suggestion that he has no desire to harm you in any way. That wouldn't be trying to erase the effects of what the doctors did to him, so I don't think that would have any ill consequences."

"When can you do it? Because I know it's not him talking, but it's still so hard to hear and it hurts, especially when he got ugly about it and started telling me it was my fault. Once in a while, I think I can deal with that, but living with him...I can't do it every day, not and get stronger myself."

"And you definitely need to get stronger," Helen said.

"I have an opening this afternoon if he'll agree," Gregory said.

"I'm sure he will. I'll call him, then he can meet us here after my session with Helen."

That afternoon, Alex met them at Gregory's office.

"How do you feel?" Gregory asked.

"Fine. I don't understand, I feel fine, peaceful even. Basia is always a mess after her sessions."

"Yours was a much more normal session. Hers have been very experimental and unusual. We're working with horrible mental tampering with her. I wouldn't be surprised if you react more like she has later on when we start working to undo the damage the doctors have done to you."

"So what now?"

"Now we wait and hope," Gregory said.

"Hope for what? That's not exactly what I want to hear from a professional."

"Alex, you must understand hypnotherapy, while an old practice, is not always precise," Gregory said.

"I know. I just wish it was, I wish you could be certain that worked and that I won't hurt Basia anymore by saying such cruel things, or worrying about physically hurting her."

"Time will tell, Alex," Gregory said.

"Is there anything else you can tell me that might help?"

"Be careful when drinking alcohol. Since it lowers inhibitions, it might lessen the effectiveness of my suggestion. If possible, I would avoid it entirely for a while. Other than that, try not to think about it too much. The suggestion is there in your mind, and if you just let it be, it should do its job."

"Should?"

"I've never worked with someone who had mind control performed on them before. No one has. So I'm not sure if that will interfere with my suggestion or not. In other words, I don't know if what the doctors did to you is stronger, or if I am stronger," Gregory said.

"And what about me?" Basia asked.

"You'll keep meeting with me," Helen said. "I'd like to see you twice a week for a little while until we know how all this is going to pan out. Then we can go back to once a week. Are you okay with that, Basia?"

"Of course, anything you think will help me, I'm definitely okay with."

"Good. Now go get some rest, and try not to fight anymore, all right you two?" Helen smiled as she said the last to show she was mostly joking.

CHAPTER 24

THE AUGUST SUN BEAT DOWN full force on the day of the trial, and Basia was a bundle of nerves. Alex had convinced her to buy a nice, new skirt and blouse to wear and a comfortable pair of new shoes so she might feel a little more confident. She had also gone so far as to treat herself to a nice haircut rather than her usual trick of trimming the ends herself in the mirror, which was good enough, but usually ended up uneven in at least one spot.

Gregory's hypnotic suggestion had worked at preventing Alex from saying or doing anything hurtful to Basia, so they all agreed to wait until after the trial to start on the other method of hypnosis for Alex. He still said rude things to her sometimes, but never as bad as before he had gone to Gregory.

Basia drank decaffeinated coffee seemingly by the gallon, hoping it would fool her brain into believing it was the real thing. She knew caffeine would not help matters because it always added to her anxiety.

When they walked into the courtroom with Mr. Templeton, she swore her heart stopped when she saw Dr. Godfrey and Dr. Schultz at the defendants' table. Dr. Godfrey gave her a small but wicked grin, seeming to say he had terrible things in mind for her when this was all over.

Alex tightened his grip on Basia's arm to help steady her as they walked to the plaintiff's table. They waited for what seemed like an eternity for the judge to enter the courtroom. Basia had seen Gregory and Helen as they walked in, but dared not turn around to look at the spectators for fear of losing what little calm she had. Instead, she stared down at the table, taking deep breaths, trying to relax. She glanced at the armed security guard a few times, reassuring herself that he would not allow any harm to come to her at the hands of the doctors in this room.

After the trial was another story, but she tried not to think about that.

You know they'll get to you somehow, even if they all end up in jail. They won't let you go unpunished, the voice in her head said.

Finally, the judge entered, then the lawyers set about making their opening comments. Basia tried hard not to listen to Mr. Templeton recount the abuse Dr. Godfrey had inflicted on her throughout her life. She was all too familiar with the horrors. She knew from their discussions leading up to the trial what he would say. When he talked of the mind control experiments, murmurs filled the courtroom until the judge called for order.

When the defendants' lawyer stood to make his opening statement, Basia's heart pounded in her ears, and the world began to go fuzzy. She vaguely heard Alex whisper in her ear, asking if she was okay, but she did not quite comprehend his words and could not have answered anyway. All she could hear was the defendants' lawyer talking about how she was a misguided girl who had suffered many tragedies in her life, and how her sanity had been affected by so many painful losses. She had a history of mental illness, proven by Dr Godfrey's notes from when she lived with him. She might believe that her nightmares and delusions were real, but of course they were not. How many times had she injured herself in the past year? How many times had she ended up in the emergency room due to her suicide attempts? The defendants' lawyer would prove beyond a shadow of a doubt that Basia required strict supervision under the care of a psychiatrist in a mental institution so that she could no longer injure herself, or worse, others.

Blood rushed in her ears at his lies. She wanted to shout at the lawyer, protest that he was lying, but knew that wouldn't help her case. She had promised Jocelyn she would make her story heard and help her gain her freedom, and couldn't jeopardize the opportunity to keep that promise. Basia fought to remain calm and tried to ignore the defense lawyer.

Dr. Tom was the first witness to be called to the stand.

"Dr. Ridgeway, why would your patient not have insisted on having a rape kit administered if what she claims is true?" the defense lawyer asked on cross-examination.

"She asked for one, but was told she would have to pay for it herself. She had no money at the time."

"Wouldn't she have found a way to pay if she was telling the truth, so she would have some proof?"

"She had no job. No home. Nothing. The police did not believe her accusations and denied her any options."

"She might have borrowed money from her young benefactor," the lawyer said, looking toward Alex.

"With all due respect, I don't believe you understand how she felt. Have you ever had to borrow money? It is not an easy thing for most people to ask under the best of circumstances. After all she had just been through, this additional injustice was more than she could handle. She wasn't thinking clearly."

"'She wasn't thinking clearly.'" The lawyer paused. "No further questions.

Helen was next to be called to the stand. Mr. Templeton walked her through her time with Basia before the defense cross-examined her.

"Ms. Federhofer, Basia lied to you about her circumstances when you first started seeing her, correct?" the defense lawyer asked.

"Yes. She was scared-"

"Please only answer the question asked," he interrupted her. "Since she admitted to lying to you in the beginning, why would you believe any of the stories she told you?"

"It is my job to help Basia to the best of my ability. If I question everything my patients tell me, I will never be able to help them."

"So it is possible that everything she told you was a lie, even after she changed her story?"

"I suppose it is possible, but I do not believe it to be. I saw the wounds on her body and the fear in her eyes. I believe she was telling the truth," Helen said.

"But you have no way to prove it is the truth?"

"Subjectively speaking, no."

"No further questions." The lawyer went back to his seat.

As the day went on and witnesses were called, it became harder and harder for Basia to keep calm as the defense twisted the truth. The transcripts of the hypnosis sessions were not allowed. Basia knew this was a giant strike against her case, since so much important information had been obtained which she was hypnotized. Alex held her hand tightly, playing his thumb over her knuckles in an attempt to soothe her.

After recess for lunch, the defense called their only witness. "The defense calls Jocelyn Ackerman to the stand."

"What?" Basia stood, fists clenched at her sides.

"Basia, please sit down," Mr. Templeton said.

Alex stood and put his hands on her shoulders and tried to gently guide her back down into her chair. "Calm down, Basia, you don't want to be cited for contempt."

Basia muttered an apology to the judge as she sat back down. When she'd suggested calling Jocelyn as a witness for their side, Mr. Templeton had immediately shot the idea down, saying a patient of a mental institution would not be a solid witness. She couldn't imagine why the defense would have called her, and worried what it would mean for Jocelyn's safety that Dr. Godfrey was back in touch with her.

"Jocelyn, you've been a patient at the Columbia Behavioral Hospital for the past five years, correct?" the defense lawyer asked.

"Yes."

"And who was your treating physician?"

"Dr. Leon Schultz, assisted on occasion by Dr. James Godfrey."

Basia couldn't believe her ears. Jocelyn had told her she hadn't seen or heard from Dr. Godfrey since she'd been transferred from Kirksville.

"Did either Dr. Schultz or Dr. Godfrey ever harm you in any way, or make inappropriate advances toward you?"

"Of course not. They're the best doctors I've ever had," Jocelyn said.

The lawyer pretended to look through his notes. "Do you recall meeting Basia Reed while you were there?"

"Yes."

"Can you tell me about your interactions with Basia?"

Jocelyn looked straight at Basia with a sneer. "She was very paranoid. When I told her Dr. Godfrey was my psychiatrist, she begged me to find someone new, told me he'd do horrible things to me. I didn't understand what she meant. She told me he'd abused and raped her when she was a child, but I didn't believe her. Dr. Godfrey had never been anything but kind to me."

"So you believe Basia was making her stories up?"

"Yes, she had to have been. But I don't know why she'd say such awful things about him."

"Did you know Dr. Godfrey married her mother after her father was killed in a car accident?"

"No, I didn't."

Basia nearly shouted out again that Jocelyn was lying, but managed to restrain herself. She'd told Jocelyn everything about Dr. Godfrey.

"Did she talk to any other patients?"

"No, I was the only one I ever saw her talk to."

"Why do you think she chose you?" the lawyer asked.

"I have no idea," Jocelyn said.

More lies! Jocelyn had been the one who approached Basia, when Basia wanted nothing more than to be left alone. Had Dr. Godfrey somehow brainwashed her?

"So she started talking to you, and told you her delusions about Dr. Godfrey. What did you do?"

"I tried to convince her he was a good doctor. But mostly I tried to avoid her."

"No further questions," the lawyer said then sat down.

"Why are you lying?" Basia shouted. "You were the one who approached me. You told me that Dr. Godfrey had done the same horrible things to you, that he tried to fuck you sane. Why are you doing this?"

"Please sit down," the judge said.

"But she's lying! She swore to tell the truth."

"I won't ask you again. Sit down, or I'll have you removed and charged with contempt of court," the judge said.

Basia sat down, and didn't even hear Mr. Templeton's cross-examination. When Jocelyn left the stand, Basia stood and went to her, and slapped her hard, leaving a handprint on her cheek.

Bailiffs rushed to restrain Basia, but she fought against them. "Why did you lie?" she shouted at Jocelyn.

Jocelyn leaned in and whispered in Basia's ear. "I did not lie. You are delusional. And in the end, Dr. Godfrey always gets what he wants."

Basia broke free for a just a moment, and shoved Jocelyn hard enough to make her fall to the ground and hit her head on a table. She appeared to be knocked out from the blow.

By then, the bailiffs had managed to get her hands cuffed behind her back and dragged her out of the courtroom, still kicking and screaming about Jocelyn being a liar.

CHAPTER 25

IT WAS A MONTH AFTER the incident when Alex was finally allowed to see Basia under supervision of a security guard, though he hardly understood why that was necessary. They had transferred her to a maximum security mental institution.

Basia sat in the chair, hunched over and staring at the floor. She did not even look up when Alex walked into the little visitor's room. "Basia? It's Alex. Do you remember me?"

She continued staring at the floor and made no indication that she had heard him.

"Can I go to her?" he asked the security guard, who nodded.

He knelt down in front of her and gently lifted her chin so she was looking at him. He stared into her eyes, and though she stared back, she seemed to be looking right though him. "Basia? Can you hear me?"

She continued staring through him.

Alex kissed the back of her hand gently and held it to his forehead.

"Alex?" she muttered.

"Yes, Basia, it's me. I'm here now." He took both her hands in his.

"What happened?" she asked.

"The case was thrown out."

"Where am I?"

He hesitated, then explained, knowing the thought of being within Dr. Godfrey's grasp again would terrify her.

"Alex, you have to get me out of here!"

"There's nothing I can do, Basia, I'm sorry. I'll visit as often as I can."

"You can't leave me here!"

"Ten minutes are up, you gotta go," the security guard called.

"I'm sorry, Basia," Alex said.

"Don't leave me! Please!" She held his arms, and he had to pry her fingers away.

"I'm sorry," he said, as he turned and walked out.

He was certain Dr. Godfrey and Dr. Schultz had something to do with Basia's outburst in the courtroom, which would mean that Gregory's hypnotherapy sessions had not been as helpful as everyone had believed. Perhaps they had even done more harm than good, as Dr. Schultz had warned Basia they would. But if that were the case, that meant it was not safe for Alex to attempt the therapy. He would have to either convince Dr. Schultz and his colleagues to reverse whatever they had done to him when he was a baby, or live the rest of his life not knowing which decisions were his own and which were orchestrated by the doctors.

Alex did not think he would be very successful with the first option. And given the circumstances, he supposed the second was preferable to what had happened to Basia. He really had loved her, and had hoped they might spend the rest of their lives together when all this was over. As it was, the case had been dismissed and Alex was left to live his life much as he had before he had met Basia. Except now there was a gaping hole in the form of a girl who could now do no more than stare blankly. Dr. Godfrey had finally succeeded in driving her insane.

THANK YOU

Thank you so much for reading *Burning Darkness*. I know your time is valuable, but if you can take a few minutes to leave a review on Amazon I would appreciate that so much. Leaving a review is one of the best things you can do to help me out, aside from telling your friends and family about my work.

My next book to be released will be the third in the Elena Ronen series, *Deceived*, and is tentatively scheduled to be released on September 25, 2014. If you aren't familiar with Elena yet, you can read the beginning of her story in *Divided* and *Ravaged*. You can stay informed about new releases and appearances at my website, www.JenniferSights.com, where you can also sign up for my email list. I promise never to spam you.